slaphappy

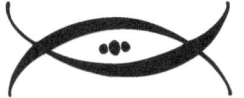

Mrs. M

Slaphappy
by ANNA WATSON

Mrs. M
by ALICIA WAG

A Lust Double

Slaphappy/Mrs. M
A Lust Double
Published by Laz-E-Femme Press
Boston, Massachusetts

This is a work of fiction. Names, characters, places and inci-
dents, are the products of the authors' imaginations or are used
fictitiously. Any resemblence to actual persons, living or dead,
events or locales is entirely coincidental.

Copyright © 2014 by Laz-E-Femme Press

Cover and interior design by Alex Jeffers,
sentenceandparagraph.com
Laz-E-Femme Press logo by Peter Wallace,
peterwallaceillustration.com

ISBN: 978-0-9960304-0-3

Table of Contents

Slaphappy Girl/Boy Smut
by ANNA WATSON

Mrs. M A book of erotic stories
by ALICIA WAG

Slaphappy

Girl/Boy Smut

by ANNA WATSON

Acknowledgements

"Victor's Secret" was originally published in *Erotic Tales 2* (Erotictales Publications, ed. Justus Roux, 2007). "September Song" appeared in slightly different form in *Only You: Erotic Romance for Women* (Cleis Press, ed. Rachel Kramer Bussel, 2012). "A Taste of Tokyo Nightlight" and "Beginner's Ass" are selections from the novel *Tasty* by Anna Watson, coming soon from Laz-E-Femme Press.

The poem Timmo recites in "Beginner's Ass" is LXXVIL—SPLEEN by Charles Baudelaire, from *Les fleurs du mal et autres poèmes*.

Thank you to my husband, Duck—she is always in my corner and is my biggest fan as well as my sexual logistics consultant. Thank you to Miel Rose, for going first and for her inspired femme love; to Sacchi Green for all the swell anthologies and for her sexy stories, as well; to my family both in Arlington and in Missoula, who love me and believe in me; and to Alicia, whose writerly companionship and steel-trap mind inspire me and spur me on. To those who are wondering about this whole girl/boy thing—not to worry! Even my straight stuff is queer.

To Duck: I am so *fucking* glad it's you!

HOW to Service-Boy up in one Easy Lesson

ord, lord, I love my job. I'm a personal trainer—at least, that's what I call it when I file my taxes—and I work for a simply marvelous establishment. Yes, when I hired on here, I knew I had found my niche. Slaphappy Productions: public gym in front, private gym in back, complete with Ladies' and Gentlemen's Locker Rooms. The clients who come to me, whether by referral or by personal choice, are looking to get in shape, certainly, but they come particularly to benefit from *my* personal fitness and expertise. In, shall we say, a rather vigorous fashion. Does your Daddy want you to look pretty taking a beating? Do your owners have a fetish for boxing or professional wrestling? Is your stamina for physical punishment perhaps a little subpar? Your pesky flinch reflex ruining your fun? Form, style, endurance—we work on all of those things here at SP; think of it as cross training for bottoms. And Luscious Louise, that's me, is the right Trainer for you! And, oh, how I glory in my role! Especially when I go to the public part of the gym to give the poor peons a glimpse of perfection, show them just how glorious a girl's body can be if she knows how to maintain it properly, and there they are, puffing away, fiddling about like morons with their weights and their trendy machines, getting themselves all in a lather. And for what? To go sit at a desk all day! Idiots! I actually get to use what I earn from my workouts, use it to take my always-satisfied clients soaring to heights previously unimagined. The dear things just can't keep away from the divine Double L., whose only wish is to remedy their defects.

Take Hazard, for example. He's been coming to me on his own initiative for the past year and a half now, determined to be the best service boy this side of the Mississippi, and truly, he is a hard little worker bee. Shaping up to be quite the boxer, too. Says he just wants to be ready for the right Lady when she finally comes along. I love all my clients, of course, as a Trainer must, but if I'm honest, I have to admit that I love Hazard just the eensy-beensiest more than the others. So you can imagine my disappointment when I got an urgent message from him recently, at a time when I was just a tad bit indisposed. He was wanting to book an emergency training session, and it was obviously very important to him, as he was practically shouting into the phone. He had a playdate, he said, with a certain Lady, perhaps even The Right One, and he wanted to do some fine tuning, make sure he was in tip top shape. My heart went pitter pat for him, and at any other time, I would have jumped to make space for him in my schedule, but, well, you see, every job has its little drawbacks, even a dream job like mine, and just at the moment I was taking some time off to recover from a smidge of necessary knee surgery. I was planning to be back soon, bitchier and trickier than ever, but for the time being, I needed to stay off the mats. At first, I thought I would have to deny Hazard the touching up he so earnestly requested, but

Lucky Lou is nothing if not inventive, and it didn't take me but a moment to devise a way to give him what he needed, when he needed it. As always, I could guarantee his complete satisfaction, as well as take the opportunity to pay homage to Cobra, the ultimate and supreme being who helped me get started in this business. All without endangering my recovery! And if I knew my Cobra, she and I would also arrange for a little private time in the Ladies' Locker Room. Just the thing to keep my attention away from the slight smarting in my knee and back to where it belonged: on dealing out humiliation and spending some quality time with a colleague whose stamina and imagination were a match for my own. Negotiations were quickly made, and the Powers That B, the triumvirate of business folk who own Slaphappy Productions, allowed me to book the boxing studio and the Ladies' Locker Room for the following evening. Perfect!

I called Hazard back and he picked up on the first ring.

"Didn't I just see you last month?" I snarled into the phone.

I could practically feel his tremor of fear down the line, and knew that he had straightened his posture and lowered his gaze as soon as he saw it was me calling.

"Yes, Ma'am, you did," he answered, flummoxed but trying not to show it. I could hear his deference, how thankful he was for my ongoing concern, how sorry he was to give me even the smallest ounce of displeasure, although for what, of course, he couldn't know.

"I thought so!" He would also never know from my voice that I was smiling. "I'm too sick of you to even contemplate touching you this week." How satisfying to hear that very slight intake of breath that meant he was getting all stirred up! "But since you're in such a fucking yank to get in here—you have a playdate, you say? Ha! I feel sorry for the poor unsuspecting Lady you've deceived into thinking you might be worth her while! It turns my stomach just to think about it! So...I'm going to throw you to Cobra, not that she deserves the insult."

Cobra, my mentor, my goddess, the only one who can kick my ass and welcome to it. She taught me everything I know about the fight and I am forever in her debt. I happened to know that she'd been nursing some bruised feelings lately, due to a slight lapse in judgment having to do with a very willing but thoroughly unreliable piece of fluff on whom she should never have wasted her time, skills, or sexual favors (but then, she hadn't asked me). I hate the thought of my lovely Cobra moping around the house, and knew it would cheer her up to come down hard on someone as hungry for it as Hazard.

I expected the boy to be on his knees right about now, thanking me for this unbelievable opportunity, but the little scamp actually found enough balls to ask for details. I took this to indicate how highly he holds me in his regard, and seeing as how he hadn't yet been blessed with making Cobra's acquaintance and so couldn't be sure of her prowess, I generously decided to disclose some personal information about the day I thought I could get one over on her. I was young, that's all I can say, young and much less savvy than I am now.

I had been working with Cobra for months, training my buns of steel right off, and I was full of piss and vinegar, felt hard as nails, and had actually started thinking I could take Cobra on as an equal and win. I was looking at it as a coming-of-age sort of thing, student beating Mistress and moving out into the world as a Mistress in her own right. Simplistic, I know! But youth is like that, unable to understand that the more complex things are, the yummier.

At any rate, there I'd be, working out in the gym, and I would start daydreaming, getting off on fantasizing about knocking Cobra on *her* ass for once. "How do you like the view?" I'd imagine myself asking her. Yeah! I would imagine the surprised look on her face, how I'd just wiped her smirk right off, then I would redouble my efforts and fucking kill the punching bag.

What can I say? I challenged her, she accepted (how she kept a straight face, I'll never know), and the big day came. I was filled to the brim with confidence, completely stoked. Cobra strolled onto the mats, looking cool and calm, her 6'2" frame radiating confidence, her eyes narrowing when she saw me. My god, she was a glorious sight! My white pride parents would be screaming race traitor at me if they knew, but Cobra's sculpted physique, her skin the color of tree bark in the rain, her hair braided like a football player, that "I will squash all comers" look on her face...damn! it was getting to me. Still does! I couldn't afford to let my pussy betray me, but I just couldn't help letting my gaze linger on her powerful arms and her bulging thighs. I shook my head to get my priorities back in line, and we squared off. I was just formulating my plan, feeling full of myself, when Cobra lashed out at me with one of her massive legs, and I went right down. She was all over me in an instant, knee in my crotch, gloves pounding my belly and tits, elbow in my throat, and then, almost as an afterthought, she laid a good one up under my chin, boxed the shit out of my ears, and that was it. Baboom. In less than a minute.

I'd been so engrossed in my memories that I'd almost forgotten about Hazard. Then I heard him moaning into the phone, probably inching his naughty hand into his tightie-whities. I recalled him to himself with a sharp command, and sternly let him know that the information I had just shared with him should, under no circumstances, give him any ideas about challenging me. He should rather look at this story from my past as one relating to a class of fighter far, far removed from his own sorry level, and that even if Cobra had bested me on the mats, I would always—always!—be able to run rings around *him*. With one—no, both!—hands tied behind my back. He agreed with such fervor that I knew I'd hit the nail on the head, and filed away the information that he'd fantasized about knocking me on my ass for use in a future session. The rascal!

The next evening, Hazard arrived at the studio right on time. He's a neat, put-together little fellow, not scrawny in the least, despite his diminutive size. He's white, but has what my granny would call "a touch of the tar brush" somewhere in his ancestry, which helps keep his complexion from being pasty and his hair from being too lank. As always, he dropped to his knees as soon as he entered my domain. I was used to the bout of nerves he contends with at the beginning of every session, but today his hands were trembling so much that Eddie, my camera man and assistant, had to help him with his protective gear as well as with his gloves. I offer my clients the option of being filmed, if they so desire, and Hazard always makes good use of this service. He studies the sessions on his own time, bless him!

"Get him up and turn him around so I can see!" I ordered Eddie, and Hazard jumped. He hadn't noticed me yet, as I wasn't in my usual place near the Locker Room door. Instead, I was sitting in comfort where I could get a good view of the entertainment. One of my other clients, the ever-clumsy Val, knelt by my side holding a tray of snacks and drinks. She was naked except for a few clippies here and there, as well as her collar and leash. She was, without a doubt, praying nonstop that she wouldn't drop or spill anything.

Slowly, Eddie moved Hazard to face me. He looked adorable in his muscle tee and clingy spandex shorts, the stretchy blue material showcasing his basket very nicely.

"Eddie, whoever said 'good things come in small packages' never saw this pathetic little boy!" I grimaced, then we laughed together as Hazard blushed and looked at his feet. If he noticed my crutches leaning against the wall by my chair, he made no indication. Oh, he really is a very good little love, not that I was going to let him know anything about that just at the moment. Eddie made sure the terrified mite was able to stand on his own, then moved into position behind the camera. That was the moment Cobra chose to barrel out of the Locker Room, her identity hidden by the fetching little Mardi Gras mask she wears when being filmed, the rest of her killer bod proudly on display in a no-nonsense bikini top and thong. When Hazard saw her, he made the most pathetic-sounding noise, something between a squeak and a gargle. Cobra looked over at me disgustedly. "This is what you've got for me to work with?" I could tell she was thrilled.

"Best I could do on such short notice, sweetie," I said. "But the young fellow has actually been learning a thing or two, haven't you, boy?"

"Yes, Ma'am!" Hazard managed to get out, then he bowed to Cobra. In touchingly formal language he offered himself up for instruction. The expression on his face was just precious: something between extreme deference and desperate defiance.

There were to be no tedious rules to this boxing match, as I don't have much use for them. Eddie, who has a nice cruel sense of timing, is allowed to ring the bell whenever he likes, and sometimes I have a "referee" or two, but today I was leaving it all up to Cobra's whim. She and Hazard touched gloves and Cobra sprang back. I was so busy concentrating on the slip and slide of her delicious shoulder muscles that I only caught what Hazard did next out of the corner to my eye. Succumbing to extreme nerves, he collapsed on the mat in a dead faint! After a moment of astonished silence, everyone in the studio burst out laughing, even Val, whose squirmy giggling caused my drink to slop over the rim of its glass. I motioned to Eddie to check on Hazard, then asked Cobra over to help me discipline my careless little madam. Hazard was going to be utterly undone when he came to, but until that scrumptious moment, Cobra and I might as well have a little fun on the side. I unlaced her gloves, then asked her to do what she would to Val, who, after that first mishap, actually managed to keep the tray from completely hitting the deck while enduring some very fierce pinching and slapping to her jiggly, voluptuous ass. I had picked her special, actually, knowing Cobra's predilection for curvy, stacked Latina girls. Myself, I couldn't keep my own hands off Cobra's death-dealing shoulders, and after a while we left Val to her own devices while we enjoyed a little Lady on Lady delight, a precursor to the after-match party I'd planned for just the two of us, in the comfort and privacy of the Ladies' Locker Room.

It took Hazard almost 15 minutes to get back on his feet, or rather, on his knees, where he begged for forgiveness for his unforgiveable lapse. Cobra, making no indication of how pleased she'd been to be able to knock out a client without even laying a hand on him, glared at the poor boy, called him a nasty, ungrateful whelp, and then grabbed him with her shiny gloves, flipped him onto his back and pulled his noggin right in-between her thunder thighs. She put the squeeze on him. I watched his bare feet drum a weak tattoo on the mat as she squeezed and released, squeezed and released. It was pure poetry.

Although she had reduced Hazard to a hot mess, Cobra hadn't even broken a sweat. She walked away, letting him drop. As he struggled to his feet, out of breath and coughing, Cobra came steaming back, bending over with her sublime ass to the camera, worrying Hazard all over as the little guy tried to regain some composure.

The abuse Cobra was meting out made Eddie cackle as he panned the camera lovingly over the scene. It was all I could do not to join in on the mats, but I really needed to take it easy so I could get my knee back in working order. To distract myself from the urge to jump in, I allowed Val to carefully place her tray on the table and then pulled her in between my own not-unsubstantial thighs for a little pussy licking to keep me in my chair. Really, I hadn't had such a good time since an old buddy of mine bought me numchucks for my birthday and a proper little karate cutie to practice on.

Now Cobra was tapping Hazard harder and harder, the force of the blows causing him to back up as he tried valiantly to keep from stumbling and falling. Finally, he managed to clear his head and even get up a little steam, blocking Cobra's jabs and reciprocating with a nice upper cut. I could see Cobra taking note of his form.

"Spunky little fucker, aren't you?" she asked, casually slapping away his efforts and getting in yet another touch. "And now, are you ready for total devastation? What? I can't hear you? Answer me, you pussy-ass, fainting prick! Are you ready to fucking die?"

Poor Hazard! He went so pale that I was afraid he was going to pass out again, but he bravely took a deep breath, settled himself more firmly on his feet, and said, quite clearly, all things considered, "Yes, please, Ma'am!"

Aw! Hazard might just be experiencing the most humiliating and painful evening of his life, but at least he remembered the manners his Mama had taught him! Cobra immediately let loose with a flurry of punches, giving Hazard no recourse and no opportunity to recover. She kept up a running commentary on what she was doing, continually exhorting him to learn from her example, to watch carefully, to get some damn education. Hazard kept belting out, "Yes, Ma'am! Thank you, Ma'am!" even as he was getting pounded, and finally, after quite a decent interval (his bruises the next day would attest to his stamina), he dropped to his stomach and sobbed out a request that the match be terminated. Cobra graciously complied, but the look on her face told me she wasn't done yet. I had a feeling she was going to take winner's privileges, and the thought made me yank on Val's hair to position her more satisfactorily.

Cobra knelt gracefully beside Hazard, whose breath caught in his throat. Surely he hadn't thought things were completely over? Surely he hadn't begun to relax? Cobra looked up and gave me a wink, obviously enjoying the sight of Val's naked and very rosy ass jutted towards her as she serviced me. That wink gave me a thrill, and I reached down to ease a clippie off Val's tit, making her scream into my pussy. Cobra grinned, then leaned over and liberated Hazard's dick, rubbing it vigorously between her big hands. Eddie tossed her a condom, which she rolled on, making Hazard moan. Cobra slapped him and he shut up. He couldn't keep himself from twitching, though, so Cobra had to slap him some more.

"And now, I think I'd like a little of this," she murmured, as if talking to herself. Releasing her grip on his rod, she straddled the nearly-apoplectic little tyke and lowered her queenly pussy onto him. Letting him feel her full weight, she smashed him under her as she rotated her hips. Hazard had that petrified "I'm going to cum but I don't know if I'm allowed to and actually I'm probably not!" look on his face. To torture him some more, I let Val give *me* a nice little cum, sighing just loudly enough that Hazard couldn't help but turn his head my way. His trembling increased as he tried to pull himself back from the brink. I cleared my throat and Cobra gave him one last leisurely gyration. We kicked our clients away from us at the same time. All this had been lots of giggles, but now it was time for the big girls to get down to business. I retrieved my crutches and followed Cobra to the Ladies' Locker Room. I would leave Eddie and Val with the task of helping Hazard come back to his senses, blue balls and all.

On second thought, I had a better idea. I turned and motioned Hazard to follow us, snickering as I watched him stagger eagerly to his feet. From what he'd told me on the phone, his playdate was a formidable Lady herself, and there was no harm in letting him get just a peek of how the big girls play. I was thinking he'd done himself proud today, and that it would be educational for him, and then I let all thoughts of him slip from my mind as Cobra lifted me up, crutches and all, and carried me over to the suspension corner, obviously aware that post-surgery protocol stipulates no weight whatsoever is to be put on the operated appendage. By the time we were both naked and I was installed in splendor, I caught a quick movement out of the corner of my eye. Hazard had gone down again! Mortification upon mortification! We'd have to do some training to help him lose the vapors, I thought briefly. Then I stopped thinking at all and just allowed Cobra to do me the way we both wanted it done. Back in the boxing studio, I could just barely hear Val shrieking as Eddie rang the bell over and over again in celebration. Have I mentioned lately that I love my job? Come down and see me sometime. You might learn a thing or two.

Loam

After work, Ted sought solace in his private greenhouse. He shed his outer shell at the door—shoes and socks, three-piece business suit—and basked naked in the damp heat and good smells of his extensive collection of plants. He might stand below the rare orchids, their sweetly anatomical flowers reaching down to him, and wait for a drop of moisture to fall into his open mouth. Or he would groom the spider plants—common and almost weed-like, yes, but he loved them, with their irrepressible urge to reproduce, always having babies, sending out feelers, ready to take over the world. In fact, Ted enjoyed tending all of his plants equally, from the cheerful, easy-to-grow annuals to his award-winning collection of notoriously finicky drosera and pinguicula. Plants, whether humble or exotic, show no pride; it is simply their nature to burst forth in beauty, and it was Ted's nature to facilitate this.

Recently, he had been asked to assemble and donate 50 planters to a fundraiser for a local shelter. He usually worked alone, but this time he decided to hire a helper. He imagined a kid, a boy who would remind him of himself when younger, to whom he might impart a few wise words, explain how the world could be good to you if you were a certain kind of man, one who kept to a certain moral code. Instead, Molly sent him her resume, or rather, he opened a dirt-smeared envelope one morning and found nothing inside but a large, green thumb-print on some handmade paper, the words, "I can help," and a phone number.

Not that Ted was lonely. Not in the least. After 40 some years on the planet, he no longer felt a frantic pull to find the perfect mate. He'd had several good but ultimately untenable relationships, and these days Ted was content with the occasional one-nighter and the pleasure of his own company.

Molly was in her mid-30s, tall and deliciously slim. Her light brown hair cascaded over her shoulders, tipped with a gentle curl. That first day, she was wearing a cashmere sweater, through which Ted could clearly see the outline of her small, pert breasts, the nipples at attention.

They worked well together from the start. Showing her how to transplant a vibrant red geranium, Ted felt the stirrings of a great pleasure. She did indeed have a rare way with plants, and was eager to learn from him. A deeply satisfying student, she had a kind of openness gained from embracing life with passion and interest. The world never failed to delight her, and Ted delighted in working alongside her. She had a pleasant voice and a knack for making him laugh. All too soon, the end of the job was staring them in the face.

Molly was sweeping as Ted packed up the last planter. He couldn't keep his eyes off her; she was luminescent in the throbbing glow of the grow lamps. Her breasts, unfettered as always, shifted slightly under her loose-fitting shirt, and her hips swayed as if she were dancing. When she looked up, it was clear she had felt him watching, and that she relished his gaze. Ted was beside her immediately, taking her in his arms, the broom falling with a clatter. They kissed and it was an exchange of energy like no other Ted had ever experienced. Why had they held back so long? Molly moaned and trembled against him, her legs giving out. He lowered her slowly to the floor. There were several open bags of potting soil under the nearest table; Ted reached out to upend one of them. Giggling, Molly helped him, and soon they had made a bed of loam, several inches deep. His need increasingly urgent, Ted tore Molly's shirt from her, feasting on her saucy breasts first with his eyes and then with his greedy mouth and tongue. He pushed her into the dirt. Licking her lips, Molly rubbed a handful of soil over her tits. This made Ted a little crazy, and he ripped off his clothes. Molly got naked as well, rolling around on her earthy bed. Ted could feel sweat trickling down his face, and Molly's skin was rosy and flushed. The air smelled of good clean dirt and the life-giving scent of an aroused woman, fertile and rich with desire. Molly gathered more dirt and welcomed his erect penis lovingly into her handful of loam. Ted thrust hard into the gritty-softness, his eyes locked with hers. He trickled some soil into her belly button and even into the drenched curls that topped her luscious cunt.

"Come on," she coaxed, lying back and spreading her pussy lips with grubby fingers. "Get me muddy."

Ted gasped as he plunged into her, the warm silky walls of her intimate insides enclosing him, welcoming him home. As he fucked her, Molly encouraged him with low moans and more handfuls of dirt, which she spread over his back and worked into the crack of his ass (he almost came when she shoved a finger into his puckered hole). When she spasmed beneath him, screaming his name, he could hold back no longer. In an ecstasy of inspiration, he pulled out, aiming his dick at her belly, which was coated with dirt. His balls tightened exquisitely and he shot, long, shimmering threads of come—more, it seemed, than he'd ever managed before—and she panted and moaned, rubbing it in, making a lovely, nasty mess. She pulled him back on top of her and they rolled, laughing, under the table of growing things.

"Stay with me," whispered Ted, when their breathing had calmed. It was full dark now, and he could see a crescent moon through the greenhouse roof. Molly nodded vigorously against his chest, and Ted was touched to feel her tears dampen his skin. Above them, orchids exhaled their lovely fragrance, and the spider plants, Ted could have sworn, looked on in riotous approval.

A Taste of Tokyo Night Life

Polly thought of Dillon as her procurer, although so far what he had procured weren't sexual liaisons but jobs. She had met him on the train in the Tokyo subway, where she was riding around, jetlagged, trying to figure out what to do and where to stay now that the friend she'd come to visit seemed to have moved on leaving no forwarding address. Dillon had more or less saved her life by taking her under his wing. He'd helped her find a place to live, and gotten her work doing all kinds of interesting things. Most recently he had found her the enviable position of dressing like a playboy bunny and selling cigarettes and gum to the audience of a music festival, a job her femme heart had swooned over. She'd made a buttload of money and as an extra bonus, had caught the attention of the person running the festival, a Mr. Inagashi.

It was hard to miss Polly anywhere, but she really stood out in Japan, with her height (almost 6 feet), her curly sweep of russet hair, and her brick-shithouse build. Dillon, an old Japan hand who also happened to be a flaming queen from the panhandle state, said he'd known a soul mate when he saw one, and the two of them had since been having a damn good time.

"The boss wants to take us out," Dillon told her on the phone. "Don't be dumb and say no." Not that Polly had thought of declining, not if there was a party to go to. She was the world's original party girl, and she would stay in Japan just as long as she was having a good time.

Dillon came to get her in his ostentatious automobile, probably the only pickup truck in Tokyo, and certainly the only lovingly restored 1945 Ford, cherry red, with a white leather interior. Polly loved riding in it, loved the way people stopped and stared, open-mouthed, as they drove by. For an exhibitionist like Polly, there was nothing better than the daily reactions she got from Tokyo-ites, who seemed never to have seen a diva such as herself before. She loved being on display. And she was damn hungry, so it was a good thing that in no time at all, Dillon pulled up in front of a restaurant. He squired Polly in, sauntering sedately under a huge crab effigy which clicked its claws with great vigor. Mr. Inagashi wasn't there yet, and Polly lost herself in perusing the menu, which, not surprisingly, featured a hell of a lot of seafood. She was trying to decide between one thing and another when Mr. Inagashi and his gang of thugs made their appearance, somberly dressed and wearing sunglasses. This was a man who never traveled alone and who, Polly was sure, must be some version of a Japanese mob boss, although Dillon denied it. Ok, she was supposed to pretend he was a regular businessman, that was fine with Polly. She decided to order the most expensive dish on the menu.

"Excellent choice," murmured Mr. Inagashi, settling in beside her and removing his shades. "I'm sure you'll enjoy it."

Polly took her first good look at him and liked what she saw. Older than most of the boys she usually went out with, he had smile lines around his eyes, an intelligent face, and thin, sensual lips. He poured her saké, ordered her meal, and made her laugh with his off-color stories about dealing with the musicians at the recent festival. The more she drank, and the more sumptuous crab dishes she ate, the more Polly fixated on his mouth, the way his lips moved. It wasn't long before she began imagining what it would be like for those lips to kiss her, move over her body, to her breasts, down her tummy, to her pussy. She gave a little shiver, and Mr. Inagashi instantly removed his suit jacket and put it around her shoulders, brushing against her. He smelled clean and woodsy, with just a hint of man musk underneath. Polly closed her eyes and breathed, then quickly opened them again when Dillon, who was sitting on her other side, nudged her.

"Don't fall asleep yet, Rosebud. The night is still young! Mr. Inagashi has a very interesting evening planned."

Polly smiled at him, shrugging. She wasn't sleepy, just dreamy.

Next thing she knew, she was back in the truck getting driven to the next place, having left Mr. Inagashi and company in high good spirits, with lots of masculine bonding and banter in Japanese much too fast for Polly to understand. She was tipsy and had no idea where they were going. They pulled into an underground parking garage, and Polly took Dillon's arm, teetering a little on her stilettos, as they hopped an elevator. As soon as the doors opened, three gorgeous Japanese women leapt to greet them, chirping a welcome in high pitched voices. The women were dressed in schoolgirl uniforms, except the skirts were so short that their demure white panties were on display. The schoolgirls seemed to know Dillon, and giggled at him, patting his chest and kissing him on the cheeks. He introduced her and she immediately forgot their names, but she smiled and nodded and allowed them to lead her over to a grouping of easy chairs in front of a gas fire. There, she and Dillon were reunited with Mr. Inagashi and his entourage, who were joking and laughing with more overgrown schoolgirls. Mr. Inagashi stood up as Polly neared, gesturing to an arm chair next to his. Once seated, watching the girls flutter off to get drinks, Polly realized she was sitting in an exact copy of the Gryffindor common room at Hogwarts, with comfortable if somewhat shabby furniture upholstered in red velvet. There were even moving pictures on the walls. Polly expected Fred and George to come bursting in at any moment (she was partial to Fred and George), or to see Hermione swotting at one of the tables. Instead, the girls came back with a tray of drinks that foamed and steamed. "Potion! Potion!" they shrieked.

Everyone took a glass and toasted each other, the evening, and good will between America and Japan in general. Potion turned out to be nothing more exotic than some kind of daiquiri.

They didn't stay long at Hogwarts, despite the wooing of the schoolgirls, who stamped and pouted as they were leaving. Dillon said Mr. Inagashi wanted to show her another bar, even more engaging. This time, the greeters at the door were extremely fey young men, topless and tricked out in mascara and clingy velvet pants. They fawned over Mr. Inagashi as well as Dillon, who was visibly more animated in this setting.

The bar itself was dim and filled with incense. There were fountains everywhere, from those tacky tinkly little things you can get at the dollar store to much more elaborate contraptions. Two entire walls seemed to be made of falling water, which immediately made Polly want to pee.

"Where's the potty?" she asked Dillon, who looked baffled a moment, then called to the lone female in the place who was mixing drinks at the bar. The bartender swaggered over, and Polly perked up, thinking she'd probably met her first Japanese butch. She loved butches—they were so gentlemanly—and sure enough, this one took her discreetly to the ladies room, displaying exquisite manners. There was even a fountain in there, not to mention purple velvet-flocked walls and toilet paper to match.

The bar was dark when Polly returned, and a spotlight was shining on a small stage in the middle of the room. Polly stopped to get her bearings and suddenly someone reached out and grabbed her upper arm. She gasped.

"Scare you?" a low, alto voice came out of the gloom. Polly recognized the butch and relaxed, shaking her head.

"The show's starting," said the butch. "Look." She guided Polly back to where Dillon, Mr. Inagashi and the five thugs were sitting on brightly colored settees in the shape of lips and high-heeled shoes. Polly perched gingerly on a pair of velvety crimson lips and turned her attention to the stage. A drag show, she hoped.

To the raucous beat of some crazy music, a young man switched onto stage, wearing a swingy skirt, blouse, and a wide-brimmed sun hat. He turned his back to the appreciative audience—almost all men, Polly realized—shook his cute little tush, then turned around again, pulled off his hat, and tossed it to Mr. Inagashi, who caught it, grinning, and gave it to one of the thugs to wear. The young man then began a rigorous and not-too-subtle strip tease, continuing to fling his garments off the stage where inebriated businessmen competed for them. Very soon, he was down to a little wisp of lace covering his nipples and a thong that barely contained his dick and balls. By now, the audience was beside itself, and Polly was totally hot. She loved gay boy stuff.

The music changed, and another pretty boy skipped onto the stage, but he was wearing a three-piece suit and carrying a briefcase. The music continued, one fast, sexy song after another, as the second young man feigned immense surprise and joy at seeing his nearly-naked co-worker. He set his briefcase down, opened it, and took out a dog's collar and leash. Immediately, the first young man fell to his hands and knees, presenting his neck. When the collar was on, the business man took his new dog for a walk, even allowing him to stop and take a faux tinkle on one of the potted shrubs bordering the stage. The audience howled its approval, and the businessman looked out at them as if noticing them for the first time. Then he stepped off the stage and began making his way in among them, stopping frequently to allow them to pet his dog and stuff money into the dog's thong. Polly couldn't stop laughing.

Mr. Inagashi patted the dog on the head and let out a chuckle as the pup went up on his hind legs to beg. After rewarding him with a wad of money, Mr. Inagashi said something to him, and the businessman led his pet directly over to Polly.

A spotlight had been following the two young men as they made their rounds, and now it stopped squarely on Polly, who was blushing and digging in her bag for some money. Just then, the dog went right up her skirt. Polly shouted with surprise, feeling the dog's nose press against her panties. She tried to push him away, but Dillon, laughing, grabbed her hands. As the rest of the audience gathered around, some with obvious bulges in their trousers, Dillon said, "You know how doggies are—just let him get a little sniff and he'll be on his merry way."

Wiggling and squirming, Polly tried to escape while the dog, his ass in the air and waving ecstatically, gave her a very thorough sniff. She knew her panties were already damp from her previous dreamy thoughts about Mr. Inagashi, and the dog was not helping as he breathed enthusiastically through the thin cloth, bumping her with his nose. Just when she thought she couldn't take any more, the dog gave a yelp and withdrew from her skirt, as the butch from the bar gave him a hard slap on the rump.

"Bad dog!" she scolded. "Not nice to go up ladies' skirts!"

The audience roared with laughter, and Dillon let go of Polly's hands. She straightened her clothes and darted a thankful glance at the butch, who winked. The men, including Dillon, who seemed extremely interested in this whole dog thing, drifted away, following the businessman who began leading the dog around the room again. Only Mr. Inagashi and the thugs (who knew, though, what they were looking at behind their dark glasses) witnessed what the butch did next. Taking the discombobulated Polly in her arms, she gave her a long, firm, utterly possessive kiss, leaving Polly weak in the knees. As her legs gave way, she was caught and held by another strong pair of arms. The butch grinned, shrugged, gave Polly one more searing kiss and a reassuring wink, then strolled back to the bar, where customers were clamoring for her attention.

"Are you ready for me to take you away from this wild place?" a voice murmured in her ear. Polly recognized the smell of Mr. Inagashi's expensive cologne and nodded. After the dog's nose on her pussy and those searing-hot butchly kisses, she was ready for anything. She looked over at Dillon, but he had two boys on his lap and wasn't paying any attention. Mr. Inagashi stroked Polly's hair and lowered his sunglasses to look at her. His eyes were smiling and lusty and she could tell he liked what he saw. The next thing she knew, she was in the elevator again, going up to the very top floor.

The penthouse was gorgeous, in a cheesy, Louis XIV kind of way. Polly dug her toes delightedly into the thick, gold-colored carpet, and rushed over to inspect the canopied bed, so high that it required a little filigreed set of steps. There was a conversational grouping of overstuffed chairs, sofa, and love seat clustered in front of a gas fire, which looked beautiful, but didn't throw out any heat. The room was air conditioned to a perfect temperature against the humid summer night, a bear rug covered the floor in front of the fireplace, and there was a full bar to one side. Mr. Inagashi provided her with a long tall glass of spiked lemonade, then excused himself. Holding her glass, her body thrumming with anticipation, Polly drifted over to the floor-to-ceiling windows, through which the lights of Tokyo spread out for miles. Engrossed in the view, she didn't notice when Mr. Inagashi came back into the room, but suddenly he was behind her.

"Polly-chan," her murmured, and Polly felt her knees weaken and her pussy clench. This was her first time with a substantially older man, someone powerful, in control, experienced. He could teach her things, show her things. And, an arrogant little voice piped up, he wants me, he thinks I'm hot, he's chosen me out of all the girls—maybe I can show him something as well! Studying her face, Mr. Inagashi smiled. He took her hand and led her to the bearskin rug. They sank down together and Mr. Inagashi began kissing her, her eyes, her throat, her neck and shoulders, darting his tongue out, making her shiver. He took his time, waiting until she was moaning for him to kiss her on the mouth, and when he did, still gently, controlled, she was panting with want, completely limp in his arms yet tingling and awake in all of her body.

"Mr. Inagashi!" she whispered against his lips, and he pulled back, smiling.

"Shigeo," he told her. "You should call me Shigeo."

Polly shivered and pressed herself against him. He continued to kiss and stroke, unbuttoning a button here, moving a bra strap there, and after a time, Polly found herself naked, stretched out on her back, quivering and needy on the silky bearskin. Mr. Inagashi—Shigeo—still dressed and seemingly completely unaffected by what was happening, got swiftly to his feet and strode off. Polly whimpered and began to call out, but Shigeo returned almost immediately, carrying a flat cloth packet, which he set on the floor beside them. Kneeling over her, casually rubbing one nipple in a way that made Polly squirm and thrash her head from side to side, he said quietly, "Polly-chan, do you like knives?"

Although Polly's sexual imagination had wandered far and wide over the course of the evening, this was not a direction it had taken. Knives? Was he using some obscure Japanese slang word for dick? No, he was now untying the black ribbon holding the packet closed, and spreading it out for her to see. A knife case, like something a TV chef might use, filled with neat rows of gleaming, super-sharp knives. Polly sat up.

"Knives?" she asked. "For...for fucking?"

Shigeo smiled, reaching out to caress a small dagger with an intricately carved handle. "Part of fucking, yes. I won't hurt you. You can ask me to stop any time you want and I will. Can I show you?"

Polly leaned over to study the knives—a blinding variety, from tiny, scalpel-like blades to some kind of machete. They were fascinating, gleaming in the firelight, radiant with a secret sexual purpose. When she looked up at Shigeo, he, too, seemed radiant, his eyes glowing with lust. Her breath quickened. She lay down again.

Shigeo nodded, snapping on a pair of latex gloves.

"Your skin is so beautiful, Polly-chan," he said, running his gloved hands up and down her arms and belly. "Turn over, darling."

Polly felt much safer on her stomach, and she allowed her legs to splay slightly, letting Shigeo see her ass and her pussy, which felt swollen, soft, and inviting. She gasped as he acknowledged the view, bending over and breathing gently there, slipping his tongue out to tickle her folds. Then he was back to running his fingers over her back, her buttocks, her legs. It was so hypnotic and such a turn on to be touched that way that Polly didn't realize when the firm pressure of his finger had been replaced by the delicate tip of one of the knives. The first she knew of it was a change in Shigeo's calm demeanor: he began to breathe more heavily and then he muttered something under his breath in Japanese. At that exact moment, she felt a trickle going down her side, and realized that he had cut her. Instead of panicking, she relaxed further. It was strange, yes, but it was also oddly soothing, and it was definitely a turn on to hear Shigeo finally surrender to his own horniness. She imagined a thin line of blood seeping out of a clean line on her back. She wanted to reach down and touch her clit, just a little, but could hardly be bothered to move. She just wanted to lie there and see what would happen next. She felt another clean sweep of blade, another trickle, another, another. He was criss-crossing her back with delicate lines, a pattern only he could see, but one which was communicating his lust to her as she lay still beneath him.

"You are beautiful, Polly-chan," he said finally, and then, with a sigh, "enough for tonight, darling. You were very brave and very good. No, don't touch yourself—get up. Come here."

Polly drew back the hand which had been creeping towards her pussy, and carefully sat up. For a moment, her head swam, but then it cleared, and she could see Shigeo sitting cross-legged beside her, his trousers undone, his hard dick poking out from the slit in his boxers, already sheathed in a condom. He was holding a glass; her mouth was very dry, she realized.

"Drink this," he put the glass to her lips. "And then this." He took her hand and rested it on his cock. Polly gulped the water, then dove onto his dick, too horny to bother with any of the little tricks she'd learned that guys liked—the flickery licking of the head, the squeezing of the balls, the teasing—she just took him deep into her throat and began to suck. Shigeo, his cool finally completely shattered, grabbed her head and thrust up, fucking her mouth hard as she moaned and drooled and held on to his thighs for dear life. Just when she thought he was about to come, he pulled roughly out, talking non-stop in Japanese—words Polly didn't recognize but knew must be filthy—and positioned her on her hands and knees on the rug, jamming himself into her as she gripped the long fleece, fi-nally just pressing her cheek and torso against the floor while Shigeo held her up by the waist and pistoned inside her. As he was, definitively, about to come, he snaked one hand around to her clit and held a finger there as she pressed gratefully against him. They came together, Polly yelling into the bear skin and Shigeo grunting and swearing above her. They crashed onto the rug together and lay there. Polly was shivering with released tension and delight.

"You're cold; I'll get you something." Shigeo cuddled her to him, then got up, stopping to lick her shoulder where blood had congealed stickily on her skin. Polly felt the electricity of that touch throughout her body, and couldn't resist reaching down to touch herself. She was a little sore, but as she moved the way she liked against her own hand, she knew she was going to come again, and come big. Wantonly, she gyrated before the fire, completely uninhibited, loving the idea that Shigeo was watching her, admiring the lines he had inscribed on her virgin back, seeing her ass move up and down, maybe even getting a glimpse of her hole.

"That's right, that's right," she could hear him encouraging her and chuckling. She flipped over on her back, eyes squeezed shut in concentration, working her clit like crazy with one hand and pinching her nipples, back and forth, with the other. The rug felt delightfully irritating on her slightly sore back as she rubbed against it. Her orgasm hit her in waves and she shouted out, "I'm coming, fuck, yeah, I'm coming!"

The last thing she'd expected was applause. Her eyes shot open as Shigeo dropped a soft robe over her. Quickly putting on the robe and jumping to her feet, she saw in amazement that the thugs and Dillon, with several pretty boys in attendance, had joined them in the penthouse, and every one of them was clapping with enthusiasm.

Polly didn't know what to do with herself.

"So this is where you disappeared to, naughty!" squealed Dillon, caressing one of his boy toys. "What do you do for an encore?"

The thugs took up the cry, "Encore! Encore!"

And Polly just had to laugh.

Victor's Secret

I was in Victoria's Secret at the mall, already half hard, when my cell rang. I knew it was my girl, Katherine, and I fumbled trying to answer quickly, nearly dropping the phone in the process. Hunched over by a display of thongs, trying to hide my boner, I know I must have looked like the biggest perv in town.

"Kitty Kat?"

"It's me, Vic." Her low voice was husky with excitement, just the way it sounds when she croons my name right before she comes. My dick stood up and saluted, and I hunched over even more.

"Where are you?" she asked, giggling a little. She knows how I react to her sexy, deep voice, and she knew damn well where I was, since we'd been planning this mall raid forever.

"I'm here," I told her, trying to sound normal, but my voice practically vibrated with excitement. "I'm in Victoria, I mean *Victor's* Secret." Katherine's giggle burst out of the earpiece, and I couldn't help grinning back, big, even though I knew she couldn't see me.

"What are you looking at?" Now her voice was serious and held a taut urgency that I could feel in my balls.

I looked around me. The mall shop was nearly empty, the bored clerk doing something with returns behind the desk and the high school girls chattering over by the boy shorts too busy with their own affairs to pay any attention to me. I started to relax a little. I left the table of thongs and went over to another display, my hard dick pushing against my khakis in a really embarrassing way.

"Well," I murmured into the phone. "Right here next to me are some really cute frilly pink bras." I reached out to stroke the seductive material. "They come with matching bikini panties, edged with lace and the back panel is completely see-through. I think they just might do the trick." I wished I could grab one, rip it off its little plastic hanger and hold it up to my face, smelling the irresistible scent of brand new lingerie. The thought made my dick jump and I gasped into the phone.

"What?" asked Katherine, sounding alarmed. I'm sure she didn't want to hear that a security guard was coming after me, wanting me to move along out of the store and stop fondling the merchandise.

"Nothing," I said in a reassuring voice. "It's just…these panties are so pretty!"

Katherine laughed, relieved. "You better get them, baby," she said. "They sound really nice." Katherine was trying to sound nonchalant, too, but her light-hearted tone belied her excitement. I knew she was as turned on as I was about the prospect of her own personal Victoria's Secret: my woman-self, that is, the Victoria who lives inside Mr. Victor Mansfield. You see, most people know me as the straight ahead, easy going, hard working systems manager that I am, a man with a pretty good fashion sense—for a guy, that is. Not quite metrosexual or any-thing, but I do keep half an eye on the better men's magazines and have taught myself to dress well. But only a select few have met Victoria, a self-avowed lingerie whore, whose smooth, perfumed body emerges from the husk of Victor like Venus on the half shell, ready to be adorned with delicate scraps of satin and lace and then to be duly worshipped.

"Victoria," whispered Katherine into the phone, sending a chill down my spine. I love it when she calls me by my girl name; it never fails to get my heart pounding and my dick hard. "You get that cute pink thing, honey. And get something else, too—something to surprise me."

"Will do," I said into the phone, practically panting. I already had my eye on some fishnets. We said goodbye and hung up. I was running my eager fingers through the stockings when I realized I'd forgotten to ask her how things were going on her end. She was supposed to be getting measured for a tux.

This little trip to the mall had nothing to do with killing time on a rainy Saturday morning; nope, we had a purpose. We were out shopping for the perfect outfits for our most important date ever—the one where we walked out in public as our most perfect selves, the ones that had, until now, been kept very much on the QT. We'd been planning this big night out ever since we'd "come out" to each other about our mu-tual love—dare I say need?—for cross dressing, and that had been pretty early on, let me tell you, since it's that important to both of us. For the big night, I'd reserved us a table at one of Boston's premier restaurants, and then we were going to the symphony. It was time to get dressed up and take it on the road, and I was both terrified—what if we ran into someone we knew and they recognized us?—and beyond turned on and exhilarated by the idea.

I'd always known I was into dressing like a woman, but I hadn't anticipated how hot it made me to fuck a girl dressed like a boy until Katherine opened my eyes. I loved the way my sexy, ultra-feminine girlfriend could use a little gel on her modern, short do, bind down her sweet bouncy breasts, change into jeans and a t-shirt, and presto! she looked like any one of the college guys who lived in my neighborhood. She even packed a realistic-looking soft dildo, something she'd found at some nasty store downtown. There was something completely irresistible about that slight bulge pressing against the fly of her 501s, something that made me want to fall down on my knees. The first time I saw her that way, I went wild. We had been enjoying a little session with Victoria, and I was wearing my favorite outfit—kind of classical, just a high-end black slip, black lace, panties, sheer black stockings held up with red garters, and open-toed red mules. For a long time, Katherine had been sitting on the bed watching me practice my runway strut, then she demanded that I pose for her. I really got off on the way she made little noises of appreciation at each new position. I was standing in the middle of the room doing a kind of Betty Boop thing, looking saucily back over my shoulder as I rested my hands on my bent knees and stuck out my ass, when Kat grabbed a bag I hadn't noticed until now, and rushed into the bathroom with a "Be right back." When she came back out, she was in complete boy drag, and she was carrying the most beautiful, sumptuous red feather boa I'd ever seen. My cock, which had already been threatening to do serious damage to my delicate panties, reared up with a vengeance. Kat strode towards me, looped the boa around my neck, and led me back to the bed. There, she pressed gently on my shoulders, pushing me to my knees on the rug. I have to say that I hardly needed any encouragement! Leaving the boa around my neck, where it draped softly, the feathers like silken kisses on my skin, she sat on the bed with her knees apart and began to slowly rub herself through her jeans. My mouth watering, I looked into her eyes, waiting to see what would happen next. Victor can be a real tiger in bed, but Victoria likes to be told what to do. Kat nodded her head, took her hands away, and leaned back a little. That's all I needed, and I was hurrying to scooch forward on my knees, to get closer as fast as I could. I began to trail the boa over Kat's fly, which caused her to gasp and thrust upwards. Then I slowly undid the buttons, relishing the sight of her Tommy Hilfiger boxers, with that delicious-looking package just inside.

"Go ahead, Vickie," Kat said in that husky voice. "Take it out. Blow me, honey. You made me so hard with your prancing around—come on, what are you waiting for?"

It gave me a such thrill to have her speak to me so firmly, and I fumbled her dick out with trembling hands. Then I got hold of myself and started to lick and suck, my brain almost going into overload as I breathed deeply—I could smell pussy as I sucked cock, and I was in heaven! Later, Kat tore my panties in her haste to get after me, and I fucked that tantalizing cunt as Kat slapped my ass and called my name, her boxers down around her ankles.

So, yeah, I guess some folks might call us rather kinky, because we found that we sure do like to mix it up. After that, sometimes we did girl-on-girl scenes, sometimes we got faggy with each other, but like that first time she wore her dick, what we really liked the best was to completely switch roles, and that was some of the hottest sex I've ever had in my life. We had so much fun behind closed doors that we finally decided to see what kind of thrills we could find cross dressing out in public.

That Saturday, we had driven to the mall separately, and the plan was for each of us to go home and get ready. Kat was going to pick me up at my condo later. I left the mall and threw my bags from Victoria's Secret, Sephora, and a couple of other very un-manly boutiques into the back seat of my Z, feeling a little self-conscious under the inquisitive eyes of the lady buckling her toddler into a mini van in the parking place next to me. What the hell—she must have thought I was a really nice boyfriend, and I wasn't going to sweat it, either. Not today, when there was still so much to do! I drove home in a big hurry.

I lucked out when I bought my condo, because it's a miracle in privacy. At the time, I was just high on the fact that I was bringing home such a fat paycheck, and I wanted something classy for it that I could show the world. A colleague recommended this Cambridge building with its gorgeous view across the Charles, and I just went ahead and got a corner unit, all puffed up with pride that I could afford it. But it turned out to be the most excellent purchase of my adult life—even better than my little Z, as much as I love her. My unit has a great big living room with two picture windows looking out over the water and into the city. It's high enough up that no one can see in and I leave the curtains open almost all of the time so I can enjoy that pretty, pretty view. I had a soft, pearl-colored wall-to-wall put in, and I even found a faux zebra rug—slick and silky—for in front of the fireplace. Kat teases me that it's a cheesy bachelor pad, but at the time, I figured that all of my frolicking as Victoria would have to be inside, and I wanted her to be able to feel comfortable and happy.

I'll never forget the first time I told Kat about Victoria. It was our third date, and we were lying on that rug she makes fun of, but she wasn't saying anything at the moment, because she was too busy moaning and panting while I sucked on her pussy. She's got the cutest pussy—exactly the kind I imagine for Victoria—very trim and neat, completely shaved to show off her shapely lips, which were swollen and flushed as I worked on her. I shoved my tongue in her hole, tickling her bud with my fingers and feeling it all in my own sweet spot. When I eat pussy with the right girl, I get the most delicious mind fuck—like I'm actually making love to myself. She came, pushing out a wild cry that might have been an attempt at my name, and then pulled me up to rest beside her. My hard on wouldn't quit, and when I felt her stirring and reaching for it, I stopped her and got up.

"I have something to show you," I whispered, and left her all drowsy and satisfied and only vaguely curious. I'd decided to take a risk—appear as Victoria without telling her first. I don't know what came over me, because usually I'm real careful, and some women I date never even get to know about my secret girl. But even right at first, there was something about Kat that I trusted. In the bedroom, I laid out a red satin baby-doll negligee with matching knickers, red thigh high stockings, my special black bra, and a pair of shiny red fuck-me pumps that I had just gotten and had been dying to wear. In the shower, I quickly shaved and moisturized, then took a last look at my man-self in the mirror. I'm not the smallest guy, but I'm careful when I go to the gym to work on stamina and not bulk, and somehow, when I transform into Victoria, I can feel the manliness melt away. The fact that my chest and shoulders are broad, my waist and ass narrow—well, that just doesn't seem to matter at all anymore.

I filled the bra with my breast shapes and fastened it on. Yes! It had been a while, and I had been missing her more than I realized. Kat's sleepy voice came from the living room, and I hollered back, asking her to wait just a few more minutes. I poured myself into all that yummy lingerie, struggling a bit with my unruly member, who was also real glad to see Victoria again and was having trouble staying out of the way. I wiggled into my new pumps, applied a spritz of Magie Noire, smoothed lip gloss across my lips and pouted at myself in the mirror. I was so beautiful. I couldn't imagine that Kat wouldn't think so, too, and I wasn't disappointed. After a moment of surprise, where she didn't know whether to laugh or blush (she did a little of both), Kat got right into the swing of it, declaring that she'd always had a thing for pretty girls. We ended up back on that rug doing 69, and let me tell you, my honey sure does know a thing or two about licking pussy. That was we started dreaming about our special date.

⋈

I couldn't believe it. I was ready: shaved, plucked, perfumed, primed. I was wearing the pink underthings, along with the filmy, backseam stockings I'd decided on instead of fishnets, which had suddenly seemed a little too slutty. Over my lingerie, I had on the quintessential little black dress, which scooped low in the back and came up to a demure halter top in front. When I walked, my breasts moved against the clingy fabric of the dress, and it felt incredible. I was wearing black Italian heels which had cost a mint, but were worth it. I'd chosen an elegant wig with a swept-up do, my make-up was flawless (the false eyelashes made my eyes look big and liquid), and when I looked at myself in the mirror, I realized I'd never felt sexier. Then the doorbell rang, and I almost fainted. I made it to the door, though, and there stood my girl, every inch the man. She's already only a little shorter than my 5'11", but the tuxedo made her look taller (and maybe she was even wearing lifts in her shiny dress shoes). Kat's hair was slicked back, she was wearing the cufflinks I had given her for her birthday, and in her buttonhole was a perfect white carnation. She handed me a wrist corsage—a divine, sweet-smelling orchid.

"Miss Victoria," she purred. "You are looking extremely fine tonight."

I blushed and giggled, hardly able to speak. My heart was pounding, but I think I managed to murmur a quick thank you, then I grabbed my wrap—a swingy, retro car coat, black with a red lining—and took her arm. She ushered me onto the elevator, unable to take her eyes off me. I was loving it! We didn't run into anyone on our way down—hardly anyone uses the elevator at my end of the building—but at this point, I almost didn't even care. Let them see! We looked really great, and I was proud to be out on Kat's arm.

After we were shown to our table at the restaurant, I could hardly sit still. My bikini panties were riding up deliciously, making me feel even more hot and bothered than I was already, and the way Kat kept looking at me—appreciative, awestruck, horny—was keeping me turned on and distracted. I didn't know if the maitre d' or the waiter noticed that we weren't exactly what we seemed to be, but it was such a classy place that we were treated with the respect and expertise given to any paying customer. I did finally calm down enough to glance around the restaurant. In the low, indirect lighting, I thrilled to the fact that we looked like any of the other man/woman couples enjoying that evening's prix fixe menu and the excellent wine. No one was watching us, whispering, or even noticing. That, more than anything in my life so far, gave me a sense of incredibly deep satisfaction. Looking at Kat's face, I knew that she was experiencing the same thing: we were passing and it felt glorious. She raised her glass, after tasting and approving the bottle of wine she'd ordered.

"To Victoria," she said, smiling. "The most beautiful woman in the city of Boston."

I raised my glass in return, unable to speak, and we sipped together, looking into each other's eyes. I slipped my right foot out of its pump and slowly rubbed it along Kat's calf. As we ate and drank, we couldn't stop smiling at each other, and I moved my foot higher and higher until my toes were resting on that wonderful bulge at the front of her dress pants. Kat shifted in her seat to allow me full access, and as we continued the meal, exclaiming over the delicate prawn appetizers, feeding each other choice morsels, I began to realize there was no way in hell we were going to get to the symphony that evening, and I was right. As soon as we had relished our last drop of exquisite chocolate mousse, we were back in my condo, too hot and too high on our success to wait another moment. But I knew that after tonight, we would be going out on the town again. Looking into Kat's face as I lay with her on the rug after our intense lovemaking, I knew she was thinking the same thing. Nothing would stop us now.

HOUSE OF L

Have I ever mentioned that I love my job? Even my recent knee surgery had its upside, because the time I spent in the hospital allowed me to do some lovely planning in solitude. And what I came up with is just beautiful. Can you picture it? A stable of knock-out, venomous girls, all under my command, all lined up and ready to offer corrective discipline and training to all the sweet, submissive clients who just can't stay away from Madame L, that's me, Luscious Louise. Yes, it was time to expand, to do a little career enhancement by acquiring a stable of my own so I could share the love. Say hello to House of L, boys and girls!

In-between visits to the physical therapist, I spent the next few months negotiating with the Powers that B for extra time and space in their state-of-the-art Gymnasium. They own Slaphappy Productions, where I have been so long and so happily employed, and were happy to give me more leeway and authority, acknowledging that I've been nothing but a shining asset to their establishment. Once that was all settled, I began training three very promising recruits. By the time my knee was almost healed, I was pretty confident in the ability of my new darlings, but before going public with the launch of the House of L, they needed to pass just one more test. Hazard came to mind. What a sweet little sub! I got a big grin on my face, just thinking about his now-nearly-nonexistent flinch reflex (thanks to yours truly). He'd even managed to almost eliminate an embarrassing (but very sweet) penchant for passing out from the strength of his emotions. He would be perfect for what I had in mind.

"I don't know if you'll be able to take the beating that's in store," I sneered into the phone. "This will be nothing like the love taps you've barely handled in previous sessions. But I will waive the taping fee if you agree to be, how shall I put it, official punching bag." I couldn't help chuckling at the thought. I heard Hazard gulp and sigh, and knew he was trembling deliciously, just like a baby girl. He thanked me kindly for the opportunity in that old-fashioned way that he has. That had me trembling a bit in anticipation myself!

On the big day, I arrived at the Gym and had just gotten comfy in my ringside seat when Eddie ushered in a scared-looking, but determined Hazard, dressed in his absolute leather best. His new Lady was of the old school, and he was beautifully done up in an ensemble that included well-worn jeans and chaps that set off his assets to perfection. He stopped just inside the doorway, his long-lashed eyes lowered in deference. Oh, it was good to see him!

"There's some more appropriate gear laid out for you in the locker room," I said quietly. Hazard jumped sky high at the sound of my voice. Lovely effect! I bit back a pleased giggle, then commanded, "Go!" Eddie and I looked at each other and shook our heads. The thing about Hazard is that you never remember the degree to which he's a such a perfect subject until you actually see him again. Really so sweet! Here he came now, stepping humbly back onto the mats. I made him do some warm ups—a genuine pleasure to take in his scrummy physique!—then pressed the button that signaled to the girls that we were ready.

Enter Sewer Rat, jogging in lightly on the balls of her feet. She looks enough like me to be my sister, with her strawberry blonde hair, Irish features complete with a few freckles, and tough-girl attitude. I'd recruited this supple sweetheart from the public gym where she'd been wasting her considerable talents on all-too-respectable pursuits. She'd been thrilled to hear that she could put her fine, muscular body, her boxing and martial arts skills, to better use.

When Sewer Rat first saw Hazard, she gave me a quizzical look, like, "This is what I'm supposed to work with?" I knew that she'd been dying to get her ratty little paws on him, ever since she'd been allowed to watch me do some training with him. She confessed that he was so much her type that she'd spent her whole time behind the one-way mirror stroking her very cute little pussy. You wouldn't know it from her 'tude now, though, as she grumbled under her breath about the poor quality of clients these days, putting up her gloves and starting to circle her prey. She and Hazard were wearing the same thing—headgear, gloves, knee and elbow pads and spandex shorts, and they looked as pretty a matched pair as you could imagine.

"What happened to you, loser?" growled Sewer Rat. "Someone throw up on you?"

Hazard looked desperately at his impeccable outfit, searching for the problem, as Sewer Rat let out a loud, rasping laugh.

She's a cutie, that Rat, and I loved to see how much fear she was able to throw in Hazard's direction. Now she was flowing through a sexy little routine, dancing around the off-balance Hazard, sending out little experimental jabs. He parried, as instructed, but I could tell he was holding back, and so could she, so she unleashed a flurry of punches. Then, giving him no time to recover, she came around with a series of beautifully executed kicks to his chest and belly. He went down nice and polite, moaning just a little bit. I picked up my bullhorn (nice touch, don't you think?) and commanded him to get up again. Everyone in the room but him was grinning big. He managed to get upright relatively quickly. I expected Sewer Rat to get right back into Hazard's drubbing, but she seemed to be kind of high on her mad little dance routines, feinting and skipping all over the mats. I reminded myself that she was still pretty inexperienced.

"Sewer Rat, concentrate!" I shouted. "Slap the little turd into next week!"

Well, that got her going. She was immediately on task, her gloves a blur of motion as she dealt out solid smacking punches. I sighed in satisfaction as I watched Hazard weave and parry, making a really good show of himself. Sewer Rat was a thing of beauty to watch as well, and I could tell Hazard was getting distracted, as he always does around powerful Ladies. In fact, he was starting to get that, "I'm going to pass out," look on his puss, but I was having none of that, not this early in the game. I instructed Sewer Rat to hold back on any knock-out punches. She was really warming to the task now, experimenting with different punishments: toe to the ribs, kidney punches, rabbit punches. I nodded with satisfaction and took a few notes in my book. Sewer Rat was shaping right up. I knew I would be able to count on her to do a professional job with the Slaphappy clients. Hazard's eyes were glazed and this big, happy grin kept breaking out on on his face, despite—or probably because of— how hard he was working to stay upright.

"Wipe that off of him!" I hollered, pounding the arm of my chair. Sewer Rat kicked his feet right out from under him, and he went down flat on his back. As he tried to rise, I gave Sewer Rat the nod. Ripping off her gloves, she dropped, pinned him, and proudly applied the front face lock we'd been working on. She really got her claws into him, and he writhed and gasped and humped up, trying to break the hold. He was pretty good, but no match for Sewer Rat, who held him almost sweetly, like a mama with a baby. I know it cost him, but he had to do it: he tapped politely on the mat, signaling his complete submission. I rang my gong, nodding. Sewer Rat had done enough for the day, and she had done it almost impeccably.

"Drop it!" I ordered, and she dumped him, stripped him of his equipment save the shorts, and strutted off, flashing me a predatory grin as she went. I took a deep breath, looked up to catch a wink from Eddie, then pressed the button for Dingo.

Ah, Dingo! Not a lot of height, but built like you wouldn't believe: 190 pounds of chiseled, rock hard muscle. Not an ounce of flab on her, no jiggles, no waste. Like every inch had been lovingly gone over by a master sculptor. She represented a special investment, as I'd actually flown her over from her native Australia, rescuing her from a dead-end wrestling career. She claimed the Australian public wasn't ready for an Aborigine super star and when I got a look at the poor excuse for a woman who took the national championship, a wimpy white blob, I had to admit something was out of whack. I promised Dingo she'd be a success in the States, at least in my particular line of business.

She came loping out of the locker room wearing just a few scraps of shiny black leather that did nothing to hide that magnificent physique. Seeing Hazard struggling to stand up, his mouth open in awe at the sight of her, she shook her head sadly and knelt by his side. She moved with such grace that it practically made me cry, and I settled back to watch the show. More experienced than Sewer Rat, Dingo knew exactly what to do.

"Having a bit of a kip, then, are we mate?" she rumbled in her deep voice, gentling his head in her huge hands. "There now, wakey, wakey!" She stroked and massaged Hazard's body, cradling him close as she tenderly kissed his face. Under these mellow ministrations, Hazard slowly relaxed. Dingo helped him to his feet and he shook his head, trying to clear it. Dingo grinned, joshing with him and giving him a bit of a tickle. Clearly off balance, not having expected more than one Lady, Hazard smiled shyly up at her as she whispered something in his ear.

"Pro wrestling match!" I announced through the bullhorn. "I'm the ref, and we're going with a three count!" I put down the bullhorn and moseyed over to the mats where I goosed Hazard a good one. He gasped, then looked at me worshipfully. I thought he was going to fall to his knees in ecstasy at my nearness, so I goosed the little sweetie again to keep him on track, and Eddie sounded the gong.

Dingo threw back her head and let loose with an ear-shattering whoop. I thought Hazard was going to pass out—it wouldn't be the first time, as we know—but he managed to keep it together.

"Put 'er right here, mate," said Dingo, guiding one of Hazard's hands to her granite abs. "C'mon, give it your best go!"

I could see Hazard gathering his resolve, obviously hating to let fly on such a magnificent and awe-inspiring Lady, but also knowing that it was what I'd brought him here to do. He looked at me, I nodded, and he took a deep breath and went for it. I could tell that Dingo was actually a bit taken aback at how good he was, but then she got fully into the game, egging him on as he made contact again and again. Hmm, something for my notes—Dingo might be a bit of a switch. Finally she grabbed him and they locked up. That didn't last long, though, and the next thing I knew, Dingo effortlessly floated Hazard onto her shoulders, him gasping in the endearing way he has. Then she started to spin him. Oh, it was beautiful to watch! Around and around and around goes the little airplane! Hazard was terrified, his eyes open wide and his hands uselessly opening and closing, while Dingo looked almost bored. At last she slammed him to the mat, firmly planted her boot on his face and looked over at me.

"One!" I sang out. Hazard lay trembling, uncertain of what to do.

"Two!" I winked at him and he gathered his strength, trying to get out from under Dingo's foot. "He got his fucking shoulder up!" I yelled in Dingo's face. "What are you waiting for?"

Dingo didn't hesitate: she picked that cute little fellow right up off the mat and held him over her head again. She proceeded to use him like a barbell, hefting him up and down a few times, her biceps bulging, her face running sweat. Nonchalantly, she flicked him high into the air, then lowered him to the mat, dropping down to cover him.

"One!" I walked around them, admiring the living sculpture. Hazard was in some kind of serious ecstasy, but he had tried to arrange himself in a pleasing fashion. He was breathing hard and I believe I could see tears in his eyes. Dingo was just smiling down at him.

"Two!" I crouched to examine things more closely and was just about to count three, when I decided it couldn't end yet. "He's up!" I screamed. "Give him your best move, Dingo! He's asking for it, the little cunt!" Dingo didn't hesitate this time, just pulled him up. He fell into her arms as she went for the the top of his head with her elbow, pulling the punch at the very last minute. Regardless, Hazard fell full length, crying in earnest now. I counted to a leisurely three.

"The winner!" I yelled, heaving Dingo's arm up into the air, and she left, with one final caress to Hazard's cheek. It was touching to see how he leaned into her powerful hand, looking up at her gratefully. I would definitely be expecting him to thank me properly later, for this very special instruction he was benefiting from today.

I got comfy in my seat again, then pushed the button for my last girl. Nightowl was a rough-looking, rangy punk babe of Japanese descent, covered in riotous tattoos and sporting a haircut that went way way beyond a bad hair day. Her style did nothing to conceal the fact that she was a classic beauty, however, with come-hither eyes, gorgeous kissable lips and tits to curl up and die on. She was wearing a Catholic school girl plaid kilt and nothing else, so you could really take the time to admire her pert rack. My Nightowl, such a gorgeous girl, and such a talented ballbuster! Before Hazard had adjusted to the change of Ladies, she was all over him, straddling him, rubbing herself up and down his compact little body, stripping off his shorts. Then she smacked the shit out of his face until he was crying.

"Please Ma'am!" he choked out finally. I was proud of how he was taking the slapping, knowing for a fact that one of the hardest things for him was to stay still for anything having to do with his face. He was even keeping his eyes open! Oh, Hazard, you really are such a good boy! I nodded at Nightowl, who did tend to go just a tad bit overboard when it came to slapping handsome boys.

"Where the fuck is your dick?" she growled in her sweet, baby-girl voice.

Hazard turned seven shades of purple, then obediently slipped out of his boxers. Nightowl looked down and exploded with laughter.

"*That*?!" she scoffed. "That is what I'm supposed to work with?" She raised her eyes to heaven and crossed herself. I couldn't help it, I guffawed at her shenanigans, all the while enjoying Hazard's plump, half-hard dick, absolutely satisfactory in every way. My jolly laugh caused Hazard to turn an eighth shade of purple. Nightowl, meanwhile, had transferred her slap energy to Hazard's tool.

"I've been in this business for a long time," she mused, yanking that thing until Hazard had to stuff a fist in his mouth to keep from screaming, and even I winced just a little. "Quite a *long* time (yank) and truly, really and truly (yank) have I never seen anything this fucking lame (yank)." After this edifying monologue, she got down to it. She released Hazard's dick, then clapped and rolled it viciously between her hands, causing Hazard to spit out his fist in a strangled yelp.

"Get up, you fucking eunuch!" Nightowl commanded, and Hazard struggled painfully to his feet. "I've seen babies hung better than you," she sneered, as Hazard swayed, mortified and more and more turned on. "You think you're a man? You call yourself a man? That offends the shit out of me, you asshole— take this! Ki-yaaaa!" Her right foot lashed out with lightning speed, striking Hazard with the heel, right in the balls. All my Ladies know how to pull a punch, but you would never know it from Hazard's reaction. He dropped like a stone, grabbing his crotch in agony, rolling around and trying not to tap out. He wanted to, bad, but the look he gave me told me he wanted to please me even worse. I blew him a kiss and he took a deep, determined breath. Nightowl got him back onto his feet and pried his hands off his crotch, screaming in his ear the whole time about what a pussy, what a wimp, what a fucking retarded slob he was. I was grinning proudly ear to ear, and Eddie and I exchanged satisfied a nod. What a show!

Nightowl held Hazard's arms over his head. That cheeky girl looked over and winked at me, then proceeded to surprise and delight me with her next move: a beautifully executed head butt, right where it mattered. It was a gorgeous thing to see my gorgeous Nightowl nut my angel right in the nuts, her crazy chopped mess of a hairdo mashing into his precious equipment. He went down so fast she lost her balance. She recovered quickly, though, blew me a kiss, and bounced out, exuding a saintly glow. My punk Madonna. What a girl! As for Hazard? He'd finally succumbed and was out like a light.

When Hazard came to, it took him exactly three seconds to realize his Lady had joined us in the studio (well, really, she'd been there the whole time, behind the one-way mirror) and just a couple more for him to be kneeling fetchingly before her. Cobra reached out and clipped a leash to his collar, then leaned over for one more kiss from me. It must have been quite clear to Hazard that, while he was out, she and I had been doing much, much more than kissing. Oh, because didn't I mention? Cobra, the bad-ass who taught me all I know and who had recently gotten up close and personal with Hazard while doing a favor for me—she was Hazard's new Lady. Yes, that's right, add matchmaking to the many talents of yours truly. Want to know exactly how talented? Just call the number on this card, sweetcheeks, and we'll make an appointment. You won't be sorry, I promise. Until then—stay sweet and stay kinky. And that's an order.

Beginner's Ass

There was a new student in Polly's advanced Japanese class, something she barely registered. People were always coming and going at Go Go *Nihon-go*. When the new guy asked an extremely intelligent question about tense agreement, however, she looked over to check him out. Timmo was from Finland, he'd said, tall with tousled jet-black hair making a contrast with his slightly pasty white complexion. His eyes, Polly saw with a little jolt, were a deep midnight blue, utterly sexy with the black hair. She wasn't too tired to think "Yummy" to herself, but it was a few days before the two actually got a chance to speak. By then, they'd recognized the fire of a passionate scholar of Japanese language in each other, and just naturally started talking about the day's lesson after class. They ended up in a coffee shop near school, where a table of less dedicated scholars—all models from LA here for a three-month gig—simpered and gesticulated, looking jealously over at Polly who was deep in conversation with Timmo about translation.

"My goal is to translate this into Japanese," Timmo said, looking meaningfully at Polly and pulling out a book from his backpack. He put it carefully on the table and caressed its worn jacket with two, delicate fingers.

His every gesture was laden with meaning, he did nothing quickly, and there was no wasted movement. He seemed to think through everything first, trimming it down to the essentials, then performing it as if on stage. His eyes were full of melancholy and his full lips expressed ennui and existential angst. He carried a French version of Baudelaire's *Les Fleurs du Mal* with him everywhere, and had already declaimed by heart several of the *Spleen* poems, which Polly enjoyed but didn't understand since she didn't know French. Now, however, he was showing her an English translation of a Finnish poet, Paaulo Saarkasi.

"See, how do you think I could get this across in Japanese?" he asked, pointing to a passage in the book.

Polly read it out loud:

You enter the room
taking the mirror, the woman, the moon: all speaking
another language, another frequency.
Their voices pierce your head
and you hear:
unleash me!

"Wow," she sighed. This was better than the Sunday Jumble, which a teacher in grade school had gotten her hooked on and which she could find only infrequently here in an English-language newspaper. "Well, first of all, you'd have to figure out what kind of 'you' to use."

"Exactly," agreed Timmo.

Soon, the two of them were meeting regularly after class, working on the translation. They monopolized the advanced class, driving out less serious students with their annoying habit of making puns in Japanese and wanting to spend more time than anyone else discussing obscure points of grammar. Their teacher began to get a harried look every time one of them raised a hand, but she gamely attempted to keep up with them by studying grammar herself in the evenings and by bringing in more and more complicated texts for them to translate.

One evening, Polly and Timmo ended up back at Polly's apartment. They had been eating at a nearby soba restaurant and Polly had been telling Timmo about the neighborhood bath. Timmo, who lived in a *gaijin* house where there were only grimy shower stalls, said he would love to check it out, so Polly invited him to go with her that night. The excited interest they shared in Japanese had recently become charged with barely contained sexual intensity.

Polly had thought Timmo was cute from day one, but she'd never been too sure how to read him, as his studied mannerisms and reserve made it difficult to tell how he was feeling. Tonight, though, his dark blue eyes sparkled as she enthused about how the experience of going to the bath, being naked with her neighbors and local shopkeepers, brought her deep into the heart of Japan. As they walked, he moved closer to her, finally putting his arm around her.

Timmo's compact, muscular form felt good moving close to hers. After seeing him safely to the men's side, Polly took her time undressing, then washed slowly, sluicing soapy water over her breasts and belly, imagining Timmo right over the partition, soaping up his own sexy body. She was too excited to relax fully in the bath, but she lingered, chatting with some of the other women floating there, one of whom she finally placed as the proprietor of the laundromat she used.

When Polly emerged, hair wet and face flushed, Timmo was waiting, his curly hair springy and damp. He looked more relaxed than she'd ever seen him. Without speaking, they returned to Polly's apartment, rolled out the futon, and undressed in the soft light from the streetlamp that filtered through the curtains.

Still without saying a word, Timmo gathered Polly into his arms, lifted her, and placed her face down on the futon. He stroked her shoulders, back, arms, legs. He seemed to be deliberately avoiding her ass, which just made it feel like her bottom was beginning to swell, balloon with desire, as he kept massaging all the other parts of her body. Finally, she began to squirm, pushing her ass out at him. When this didn't work, she tried to roll over, but he stopped her firmly, then, without warning, he smacked her butt with the flat of his hand.

Polly yelped and tried to turn over again, heart racing. She'd never been spanked, never even thought about it, and she wasn't sure she wanted him to do it. But Timmo kept raining down the blows, almost mechanically, covering every part of her cheeks, and after a while, Polly found she didn't mind after all. It was hypnotic, almost, and she began pushing herself up to meet his hard hand, whimpering into the pillow. It hurt, but it hurt good, and it was taking her out of her head and into somewhere else, somewhere where just the body lived, ripe and wanting.

Now Timmo was making small grunts of satisfaction and the sound of his breathy voice combined with the rhythmic slapping, was making Polly incredibly turned on. Her pussy was completely drenched and all she wanted was for Timmo to roll her over and plunge into her, fuck her hard, but that wasn't what seemed to be on Timmo's mind. He continued to torture her ass, slapping, pinching, rubbing, kneading, until her cheeks were on fire and she was starting to cry with the conflicting feelings of pleasure and pain. Still, she was determined to take it—she didn't know why, exactly—it was almost as if she wanted to prove something to him. She buried her face deeper into the pillow and held on.

The pounding slaps continued for a long time, and even longer. When they stopped, Polly hardly knew what to do with herself. She thought she might float right up to the ceiling, maybe even pass right through it and out into the Tokyo night. Timmo rose and she could hear him rustling around in his backpack, but she was too flummoxed and snotty to raise her head to see what he was doing.

"He's busy," she thought, wiping her eyes and nose on the pillow.

She concentrated on slowing her breathing, managing to get so relaxed that she was almost dozing when Timmo gently touched her on the ass cheek. She jumped and drew in her breath. It was so sore! Timmo now had his hands on both cheeks, pulling them apart. Polly blushed, thinking of him looking her asshole, examining it in his calm, dispassionate way, but she still couldn't bring herself to move. She had been spanked into immobility.

Something cold dripped down her crack, and she gasped again as Timmo smeared the slippery liquid all around. A finger found her hole and began to tease it open. Polly could hardly believe what was happening. It felt so good, she never could have imagined! She knew people did this, of course, but it had just never come up before.

She pushed back onto Timmo's finger experimentally, and he made a pleased noise.

"Open, open," Polly chanted to herself.

Soon, Timmo's entire finger had been sucked in and he was beginning to move it, tickling her, coaxing her wider. He squirted on more lotion and then had two fingers in her. She spread for him, lost in the feeling of fullness. Her clit was throbbing, but Timmo paid no attention at all to the front of her body, as if her breasts, belly, and pussy didn't even exist.

"I am ass," thought Polly giddily.

Suddenly, Timmo pulled out and Polly moaned. The feeling of emptiness didn't last long, however, as soon the head of Timmo's dick was knocking at her back door.

"Ooh, yes, Timmo, do it!" Polly whispered, and then he was in her to the hilt, heavy and still, his full weight pressing down on her and he was speaking at last.

"*Je suis comme le roi d'un pays pluvieux,*" Timmo intoned, beginning to move in increments "*Riche, mais impuissant, jeune et pourtant très vieux.*"

Baudelaire again. His breath tickled her ear as he spoke the incomprehensible French words. Polly felt impaled, like shish kebob. Timmo's dick felt so big in her ass that she pretty much expected him to be coming out the other side. At the same time as she was paying attention to these things, she was also completely elsewhere. She began making noises she'd never made before during sex, a kind of keening wail, sharp squeaks and splutters, deep, chesty huffs.

"*Rien ne peut l'égayer, ni gibier, ni faucon, Ni son people mourant en face du balcon.*" Timmo continued to recite, his voice amazingly calm, even as he increased the pace, his dick throbbing and alive inside her.

Polly urged him on, humping up at him, calling out random words in English, Japanese, even Greek. Feeling him begin to strain against her, she reached down and touched her clit—it only took a few hard strokes—and the two of them were both coming, Polly screaming, "*Chikushyo!*" and Timmo grunting through the last part of the poem.

"*Il n'a su réchauffer ce cadavre hébété, Où coule au lieu de sang l'eau verte du Léthé.*"

The final line came out almost in a whisper, and then he slumped on top of her, his cock twitching, emptied into her ass. Still he didn't turn her over, just lay there on top of her, keeping her pressed into the futon. Eventually, they fell asleep like that.

When Polly woke up, it was the middle of the night, and Timmo was gone. Unable to get back to sleep, her ass sore, her mind full of what had just happened, she stumbled around muzzy headed making herself some coffee. Sitting at the table with her favorite mug, she noticed Timmo had left his copy of the Saarkoski book behind. She pulled it towards her and opened it to the first page. Timmo had written something there; she had to squint to make it out as his handwriting was miniscule. It was in Japanese.

"To a delicious piece of ass who will live forever in my memory. I'm moving on to keep a rendezvous with a friend in Thailand. Think of me when you read these poems, keep on with the translation. And come visit my gloomy country some time."

He'd included an address in Uppsala. Polly closed the book and sipped her coffee, staring out the window at the Tokyo night, which never got completely dark. She would miss her scholarly sessions with Timmo, but she was quite sure she could convince any number of people to carry on where he had left off, sex-wise. She grinned to herself, finished her coffee, and went back to bed.

september song

Ruthie reached down and quickly adjusted her thong. Sol saw her and winked. He was sitting in the armchair, dressed in a suit, knees apart, hands resting on his cane. His trousers were tented from his hard on, and Ruthie wished she could crawl over there and dive on it, but he didn't want her to stop. Said he was enjoying the view too much. She straightened up, her naked breasts swaying, and continued reading from Duke Ellington's autobiography.

"Roaming through the jungle, the jungle of 'ohhs' and 'ahs' searching for a more agreeable noise, I live a life of primitivity with the mind of a child and an unquenchable thirst for sharps and flats."

She paused again and looked over at Sol. His eyes were closed and one hand had left the cane and was resting on his penis. She wiggled uncomfortably as he murmured for her to go on. She was a novice thong wearer, and it certainly took some getting used to. Still, what better way to spend a rainy afternoon than listening to old jazz on the stereo and reading to your lover in the near nude? She licked her finger, turned the page, and went on.

Ruthie and Sol had met a year ago after Ruthie had made a pact with herself to spend some of her time giving back to her community. She signed up with Lend A Hand, a local organization matching volunteers with nonprofits, where they asked her to be a clothes-runner. Her job was to take the used clothes Lend A Hand provided and distribute them to clients at City Eats, a free meal held at a local church. All she had to do was show up with her jeepful of clothes every week and hand them out. Some of the people who came to eat were on the street, some of them just down on their luck or on a tight budget. She wasn't sure how she would like it—she had been hoping for something involving children—but it turned out to be a lot of fun. After a few weeks, she started to get to know some of the regulars, like Ellis, from California, who loved interesting t-shirts, and Darla, who was missing most of her teeth and liked scarves. Ruthie found she enjoyed talking to folks about what they would wear if they had the money, and then trying to find it for them, either in what she got from Lend A Hand or on her own, at thrift shops and yard sales. She was especially proud when she found a leather jacket for Sol, even if it did have a small stain and an even smaller tear.

"I have sartorial sense," Sol told her the first time she showed up at City Eats. He had come right over and started going carefully through the clothes. He wouldn't take just anything. He was a big old man with clear gray eyes and a hawk nose. Around 75. "Can you get some good quality things?" he'd asked. "Can you find some nice threads for this old man?" He looked at her with those gray eyes and smiled. He had all his own teeth. Sol was old, but he was pretty well preserved. Ruthie told him so, and he kept smiling, taking her in, leaning on his cane. One made out of dark wood; very manly.

Soon, Sol became her unofficial helper. He would stand beside her holding the sock bag, for example. When they bumped shoulders or hips, Sol would gravely say, "Excuse me, young lady."

"This is a good story," said Sol one evening. "Let me tell you this story." They were sitting eating together in the church basement, keeping an eye on the clothes table. Ruthie put down her forkful of macaroni and cheese and looked at Sol expectantly. She loved it when he told stories.

"I was about 14," Sol began. "And I had saved up enough money to get a radio for myself. I went to Jordon's and got a good one. I was proud of that radio. Right after I got it, I was listening to Bob Hope, and at the time, hemlines had been going up, you know, women's skirts. And so he's telling jokes, patter, and he says, 'Well folks, the way I see it, if ladies' skirts get any shorter, they'll have more hair to comb and two more cheeks to powder!' and just then, the radio went dead. I jumped out of my chair—I thought my brand new radio was broken. But of course, they'd pulled him off the air. I heard he got a fine."

Ruthie was laughing. "I can't believe that!" she said. "Did you get the joke?"

"Get it? Of course I got it! I was 14 years old!" He looked offended.

"Well, some people are still pretty naïve when they're 14," said Ruthie. She put her hand on his arm and left it there.

Sol had a special kind of smell. It was his clothes, Ruthie thought, because in general, he seemed pretty clean. Well-shaven. The smell—dusty and metallic—came from being outside in the city all the time, sitting here and there on the

T, reading the paper someone had left, working the crossword, looking in the trash for bottles and cans. He was always out, always walking around. Slowly, of course, with the cane.

It wasn't long before Ruthie started taking home some of Sol's clothes to wash and mend. As she shoved them into the washing machine, the smell would surprise her, and she would smile. She had the feeling that if she were to put her nose right up to one of the benches on the Cambridge Common, it would smell just like Sol.

One night, after she'd been distributing clothes for about three months, some of the City Eats volunteers asked her out with them. Usually, she sat and talked with Sol, but he'd already gone home—he had a rent-controlled efficiency somewhere—so Ruthie said yes. The volunteers were all really young, kind of a wild bunch, with interesting hair and piercings and tattoos. There was a lot of flirting and personal drama, but not with her. Someone pushing 40 was not so relevant, apparently.

As they walked to a nearby bar, the boy who wore his red hair in two little antennae turned to her. "So what's going on with you and Sol?" he asked. "I saw you slipping him a box of oatmeal. People are talking."

Ruthie looked at his shoes. That kind of shoe was very popular and didn't often get donated. "We're buds, I guess," she said.

"Oh!" said the Grateful Dead tie-dye girl. "He's such an old dear! He's one of my favorites!"

The next time Ruthie saw Sol, she asked him out for ice cream, which was something they never had at City Eats. When the clothes had been picked over and put away, Sol hauled himself up into her jeep and she drove to Toscanini's in Central Square.

"I'm paying," said Ruthie, and Sol accepted in the gracious way he had. They sat at a tiny wrought iron table. Sol's lips, thin and expressive, looked good covered with coffee ice cream, and then he licked it off, and that looked good, too. Ruthie leaned forward, showing off her breasts. These days, she'd been wearing low-cut shirts whenever she saw him. She had been feeling so sexy lately.

"You're a beautiful man, Sol," she said.

"Ruthie, I knew you were a *mensch* the first time I saw you," he replied, taking in her cleavage. He was wearing his leather jacket of course, had always worn it since she'd gotten it for him. She'd never seen him take it off. At his feet was a well-worn plastic KB toys bag, opaque, with handles, filled with cans, she thought, and maybe a newspaper.

After that date, Ruthie couldn't wait to get Sol to come home with her. She didn't have any roommates and they could be alone. This was a very alone kind of thing, anyway. She felt awkward talking to her friends about her feelings for Sol. When she tried, Trisha, a fellow secretary at Harvard who was usually pretty open minded said, "You have a crush on an *old homeless guy*? Are you *OK*?"

"He lives somewhere," muttered Ruthie, but she kept her mouth shut after that.

Sol didn't want to come over at first. He had his life, his routines. Going to Ruthie's, keeping company with a young woman, he wasn't used to it, he told her.

"You could get used to it," she said. She knew he wasn't married or anything; she'd asked. She invited him for supper on a Saturday night and wouldn't take no for an answer.

Sol showed up with a bottle of wine. He left his bag beside the door. He took off his coat and Red Sox cap, revealing a head of thinning gray hair. He was wearing a nice sweater that someone had given him, and when she complimented him on it, he lifted one arm to show her where there was a hole. She told him to take it off so she could fix it. When she took it from him, their hands touched, and she squeezed gently; he had arthritis pretty bad in his hands. He squeezed back. The mend job came out a little crooked, but he appreciated the effort.

"How little we know, how much to discover..." he sang as she got the food ready. The crooners, the big bands, that's what he liked. That's what he'd bought the radio for when he was 14. Beautiful ballads like "Strangers in the Night".

After supper, Ruthie went to the freezer and got dessert.

"I love ice cream," said Sol as he spooned it up.

Ruthie smiled. "I know." She leaned over and licked some from his lips.

"I've been wanting to do that ever since Toscanini's," she said. He sat very still. She left her chair, knelt beside him on the floor, and put her head on his lap. At once, she felt his big hand on her hair and he stroked and stroked. She moved between his legs and pressed her body against his chest and belly and crotch. She reached up under his sweater and felt his nipples through his thin undershirt—they were sagging some, but so what. We all sag eventually. She put her hand on his belly and felt the hair around his belly button. She moved her hand and Sol sighed.

"It feels good when you rub," he said softly, so she rubbed there, and then she rubbed lower. "You'd better stop. I don't know what will happen."

She looked up at his face. He was an old man. His cheeks were red, covered with tiny broken capillaries, and his eyes watered.

"I'm an old man," he said, and Ruthie said, "But can you still get it up?"

Sol closed his eyes in what Ruthie thought at first was pained embarrassment. He didn't like it when women at the meal swore or talked dirty, but then he started laughing, so Ruthie took off her shirt.

Ruthie had big tits. Double D's. It had taken her a long time to make peace with them, just about all her life. Years of baggy shirts and glaring at guys who couldn't seem to talk to her face. But now she felt fine about the way she looked.

"Baby, you are stacked but good," Sol said as he reached for her bra. "You do this. I can't manipulate too well anymore."

"But you did once upon a time," Ruthie said, undoing the clasp for him. "You had them begging for it."

Sol smiled, but kept his mouth shut. Some things were private. Ruthie came up close and rubbed her breasts on his chest and belly. She wanted him to take off his sweater and shirt, but he wasn't so sure.

"You might not want to see this," he said.

"What?" she asked. "A scar? A blemish?" He shrugged and took them off. The hair under his arms was white. She wanted to lick it. She was big into licking.

"I'm an old man," he said again, and she laughed.

"I'm going to lick you under the arm," she said, and she did, which meant her tits were banging up against him. She pushed them together and rubbed them all over his mouth and nose and eyes. He put his arms around her and slid his thumbs under the waistband of her jeans, starting to push them down. She helped him and now she was naked.

"Put your arm," she said, pulling his arm between her legs. She moved down until his hand was right at her pussy. He gently rubbed her slit, pushing up, sliding back, then dabbling two fingers in her hole.

"Ah, Jesus," said Sol, leaning way back in his chair as she held herself up on his shoulders and moved around on his hand. "So wet." He grabbed for a nipple with his mouth and they started to overbalance.

"Come to bed," she said, slipping off him. He had to pee first, and then he sat on the bed looking shy. Ruthie straddled him and pushed him back.

"I don't care if you get hard or not," she said, trying to take off his pants. Finally, he let her. He smelled like Boston. They lay on their sides, facing each other, and she kissed and licked him all over. He lay there and let her, breathing hard, sometimes reaching out a hand to touch her leg or breast. He was very white, flabby, but hard underneath, and she grabbed handfuls of his ass and just squeezed. His nice plump dick jumped in the bush of white hair. She held it and it jumped again. Sol said, "Jesus," and started pumping. Ruthie wanted to ask how long it had been since he'd last fucked, but it didn't seem very polite. It seemed a little triumphant. She took his hand and brought it to his dick and they played together until he was hard. She grabbed a rubber from the drawer in her nightstand, got it open, and put it on with her mouth. He held her head and seemed to be settling back to get blown, but she slid back up his body, licking as she went. For her, it had been a while.

His dick slipped in so sweetly, and the two of them started moaning and talking. "Fuck me, fuck me," Sol whispered, surprising her. She'd never heard him use an obscenity. She tried to keep as much weight off his body as she could, but now he was grabbing at her and pushing up. They fucked like that until he came and fell out. She just kept going on top of it. She liked the feel of it underneath her, sometimes hitting her just right. He moved his hips, his hands on her waist, helping her. She cried after she came, which sometimes happened. That night, he stayed with her. He snored.

In the morning, she cooked him breakfast, and he left, kissing her, stroking her face before shuffling off. Ruthie got a cup of coffee and went back to bed with the paper. She would be seeing Sol tonight at City Eats. They would distribute clothes together, sometimes bumping hips or shoulders and Sol would say, "Excuse me, young lady." They would sit down and eat together, knees touching, laughing at nothing, looking into each other's eyes like lovers do.

Mrs. M

A book of erotic stories

by ALICIA WAG

Acknowledgements

Thanks to the journals and anthologies that first published some of these stories. They include *The Mammoth Book of Erotica* ("Magmadootch"), Cleis Press's *Best Women's Erotica 2006* ("Consuela"), *Just Watch Me: Erotica for Women* by Violet Blue ("Consuela"), *Clean Sheets* ("Magmadootch" and "Mrs. M."), and *Three Pillows* ("Jailbreak"). This book wouldn't exist without Laz-E-Femme Press and my partner-in-smut, Anna Watson, a stellar colleague and dear friend. I'd also like to thank Rachel Maines for writing "The Technology of Orgasm," the amazing scholarly work that inspired the story "Mrs. M." Most of all, I'm grateful to family and friends for their love and support.

"(Sex is) a part of nature. I go along with nature."
—MARILYN MONROE

Magmadootch

The first time I saw Roger, he was making silly faces and stupid gestures with his hands. "Who's that?" I asked Sophie at our end-of-summer party, celebrating the return to our last year of grad school.

"That's Roger," she answered. "And the magmadootch."

"Huh?" I wasn't attuned to funny stuff. In my creative pursuits, I concentrated on technique and convention. In my deep, dark subconscious I had a proclivity for melancholy and tragedy. I liked expressionist paintings, and Kafka was my favorite writer. When I laughed at things, they usually involved irony and sarcasm. Magmadootch? It sounded like some newfangled product to clean penis scum.

"It's his pet," replied Sophie, alluding to the movements of Roger's hands, his fingers folding and flitting about in the shape of a creature's face. "The kids at camp loved it."

So that's where she met him. Sophie summered as a camp counselor in preparation for her career as an art therapist for special needs children. I'd spent the last two months immersed in music, blowing my brains into my flute at one festival after another.

"Come on," Sophie said. "I'll introduce you."

I didn't think I wanted to be introduced to a clown, but Sophie was dragging me. "Slow down," I said. "I'm gonna spill my drink." My drink was seltzer with lime. Roger's, I saw as we approached, was one of the martinis Sophie had insisted on serving. He turned from his conversation with Frank, our buddy from the running club, and smiled.

His odd grin triggered a twang in my gut, which I ignored. I couldn't possibly be attracted to such a motley man, with skin like a Mediterranean olive, unruly black curls, a nose that wasn't so much long as it was pointy, and dark, slightly asymmetrical eyes. "Roger," said Sophie, "This is Lisa."

Roger repeated my name, drawing it out in a sing-song, a-ha kind of way, saying it as though he knew all about me. "Pleasure to meet you," he added.

Out came the magmadootch hand. I shook it, surprised by its grip, which was both firm and relaxed. "Hi," I said.

We stood silent for a few moments. I felt awkward in the dead air, though my glance at Sophie indicated she was amused. Roger looked unperturbed, but then, why wouldn't he be? Anyone who would wear a striped stocking cap and red suspenders to a party must not care what anyone thought of him. That twang in my gut came back, almost like a longing.

"Oh, there's Patty," said Sophie. I nearly panicked when she left, though I could have easily followed. Instead I stayed with Roger, feeling confused, compelled, and altogether uncomfortable. The apartment was cramped with people, the din of talk and music blaring, some rock band I didn't know the name of,

I didn't keep up with that stuff. Classical music was my thing, and I didn't go beyond it.

Roger kept looking at me in a mellow, sweet sort of way. I was amazed by his lack of self-consciousness. Meanwhile, my own need to break the silence was growing so strong I was on the verge of sputtering. He seemed to know this, and helped me out. "Sophie tells me you're quite the flutist." Even though he had to speak loudly to be heard through the noise of the party, his voice had a soft quality I liked. I shrugged. "Who's your favorite composer?" he asked.

I settled a bit, relieved at the easy question. "Mahler."

"Ah, yes," he said. *"Das Lied von der Erde.* Hauntingly beautiful."

A kindred spirit. Maybe. "I love that piece."

"I like it," he said. "Not as well as Shostakovich, though."

"He's a favorite of my lover's," I said, not knowing what came over me. Dante was long gone, studying cello and practicing polyamory in Italy.

Roger's gaze never wavered. Those dark eyes staring into me must be breaking down my sanity, I thought, or was it remembering Dante and all the Italian women he might be fucking? Roger leaned in a little closer, a miniscule, almost imperceptible distance that was enough to fuel the longing in my belly. "What's your lover's name?" Roger whispered.

"Dante," I said.

"Ah," said Roger as though he had just learned something important. "A man."

I nodded. "And what are you?" I asked.

Roger took the two fingers of his right hand, the mouth of the magmadootch, inserted them into his martini, and clamped them around the green olive inside. Out they came, the olive cradled between them. He popped it into his thin-lipped, wet mouth and ate it with quiet gusto before he answered.

"Me?" he said. "I'm a mime."

⑂

Roger left the party alone, as he had come. Sophie told me he lived in a nearby suburb, as caretaker of a historic house and its grounds. "Free rent," she said.

"What did he do at your camp?" I asked.

"He did mime with the kids. You like him, don't you?"

"Of course not," I snapped. Sophie just laughed. After a barely respectable second of restraint I asked, as casually as possible, "Where does he perform?"

"He gigs around, and teaches. He's on the street a lot," she said, "in the square."

One night I wandered there, looking for Roger among the singers and jugglers, but he was nowhere to be found. As it turned out, I didn't have to look again. He came by in the middle of the week. I opened the door, on my way out to buy books for the semester, and there he was, arm raised, hand in a fist as though he were about to knock, even though we had a doorbell. "Hey," I said.

He dropped his arm and smiled. "Hi." He was wearing a cap, two-toned with black velvet and a purple, satiny material.

Another awkward silence. Roger seemed to enjoy them. I broke it by saying, "Sophie's not here."

"I didn't come to see Sophie," he said, leaving the words and their ramifications hanging. I found myself settling into the quiet. The need to find something to say was lessening, and that was nice. After a moment Roger said, "Would you like to come over tonight?"

"Yes," I answered without thinking.

"Okay," he said. "I'll pick you up at seven thirty." Then he smiled and put his right foot forward, pivoting in the most extraordinary way, every sinew and muscle working as efficiently as possible to turn his body and walk away from me.

⫸

We got into Roger's old, rickety Saab convertible at 7:37. The interior was torn up, but Roger had the seats covered with a cheerful red and white Hawaiian print. I had just showered and thrown on a T-shirt dress. My brown curls were still wet, but quickly drying in the breeze.

We traveled in silence for what seemed like forever, until Roger pulled off the highway, drove down several increasingly remote roads, then finally parked on a dirt path and said, "We're here." Above us the world looked fiery and brilliant, orange streaks and pearlescent clouds giving way to the night sky. In the distance I spied a large, handsome farmhouse.

Roger got out of the car and walked around to my side, opening the door for me. I felt like a lady in an old-fashioned movie as I emerged, demurely, instinctively taking the hand Roger offered then slipping my arm through his as we made our way to the house. "It's so quiet," I said, listening to the sounds around us. "Is that frogs?"

"Yes," he said. "There's a pond on the other side of the house." I smiled, thinking of when I was a girl, walking to the pond in my neighborhood and watching intently for tadpoles, dragonflies, sometimes even a blue heron.

Roger had a room downstairs with a kitchenette and bath, separate from the rest of the historically preserved farmhouse. It was like stepping into a different world—from austere 19th century simplicity to quirky modernism. The bed was a single futon on the floor covered with rumpled blue sheets and multicolored, tassled pillows. Charlie Chaplin stood on the back of the door, courtesy of a fraying life-size poster. Randomly and haphazardly placed postcards from all over the place decorated the wall, vintage photographs of movie stars, and art cards of some of my favorites: Wyeth's "Christina's World," Rousseau's "The Sleeping Gypsy," and Dali's "The Persistence of Memory."

"Sit down," Roger said, gesturing to his futon. It might have been presumptuous to immediately direct me to the bed, but the only chair was a swivel stool at an old wooden desk in the corner, covered with mounds of papers, envelopes, and candles.

I kicked off my sandals and sat cross legged on the futon, noticing tinges of familiar smells in the air—patchouli, sandalwood, pot, cucumbers. Roger took off his cap. His dark ringlets flew free in all directions, like wild vines seeking territory. Without the hat he looked serious, more grown-up. He methodically pulled down one suspender, then the other, unclipped them from his black jeans and hung them on a nail, then he took off his white T-shirt and tossed it into a pile with some other shirts. Is he going to strip, I wondered, as he leaned over and unbuckled his Tevas, kicking them aside. But he stopped there. He wasn't as hairy as I thought he would be, which I liked—just a tuft of black in the center, where his heart might be. His nipples were dark and hard, and beautiful. He wasn't well-muscled, but he was taut and elegant, almost feminine.

"Do some mime for me," I said. I watched as he created an imaginary table and served himself tea. "How do you make it look so real?"

"It is real," he said. "Come here." I got up and stood beside him. "See this wall?" He gestured into the empty space in front of us.

"No," I said.

"It's here." One palm, then the other, walked up the wall of air, looking for a way out. Roger pressed one hand firmly onto the surface, and took my arm with the other. "Feel it," he said.

But when I put my hand there, my fingers slipped right through.

◦

Later, when we were kissing on the futon, our lips sliding against each other and our tongues intertwined, I reached for the hard cock I could feel pressing against me through our clothes. "No," Roger whispered, and stood up.

I watched as he reached for something imaginary, something tender. "This is your breast," he said, cradling roundness, gently squeezing, finding the nipple and placing it between those two agile fingers. "I'm going to suck it," he whispered, leaning forward with mouth slightly open, closing around the exact spot his fingers had been. I watched his mouth lap at the place that was my nipple, tug at it gently with teeth, dart at it with tongue.

Meanwhile, his magmadootch hand slid down my imaginary belly, I could almost feel it brush my very own skin as it traveled lower, the two fingers dipping forward, and I let out a moan. "This is your pussy," he said, working at it with his fingers. "It's wet."

His fingers pushed forward, slipped inside, his thumb staying behind and working the pretend clit. Between my legs my real pussy gushed. "It's so wet," he said.

He let go of my imaginary pussy for a moment to pull off his black jeans, leaving his navy blue boxer shorts on, taking his cock out of them and pulling the fabric back so that his balls were exposed. It looked like a portrait—erect cock against dark background. I stared at it, the thickness and slight curve, the dark brown oval of a birthmark along the shaft that looked like a splash of chocolate. "I'm going inside you now," he said, moving forward. He held his cock in one hand and rubbed it against the clit and lips for a moment, his eyes watching my imaginary pussy as though looking at something amazing and beautiful.

"You are so ready to be fucked," he said. He slid his cock toward the entrance of my pretend pussy, slowly, tauntingly. "Fuck me back, Lisa," he said, bringing his sex up again and rubbing the head of his cock on my imaginary clit. My real clit was swelling the way it only did when my vibrator touched it. "Come on," he said. "Fuck me with your wet pussy."

I slipped off my underwear and pulled up my dress, then leaned back against the pillows on the bed and spread my legs wide.

"Now," he said. "I'm putting my cock inside you." It slipped into the imaginary hole. My eyes could see his shaft, yet I knew it had disappeared into a moist, dark chasm. Roger's head was back now, he was moaning softly. "Can you feel it?"

"Yes," I said, reaching for my clit, sliding my fingers inside myself, all hotness and cream. I could feel Roger's cock, the pressure it made in my cunt, my cunt walls stretching to welcome it. Roger pushed all the way into my imaginary pussy, and my own hips pushed back.

We started slowly, then upped the rhythm. I watched his cock fucking the pretend pussy, my hips thrusting along with it.

"I'm going to come," he said.

I felt the bud of my clit explode and pulse at the moment Roger's cock released white liquid into the air, onto the exposed wooden floor in the space between us. He collapsed on his knees and took me in his arms, hugging me so tight I almost couldn't breathe. He whispered my name, kissing my hair, my sweaty forehead, my eyelids, my lips.

I looked over Roger's shoulder at his room, the candles, the posters, the colors. It looked like a Klimt painting, and we were in it, wrapped around each other in bright fabric. Being on the inside wasn't scary the way I thought it would be. There were edges, after all. I lifted my hand and placed it against them, tracing the space Roger and I occupied.

Roger's breath streamed warm and moist on my neck as my hand, having found the borderlines, circled and guided him inside me.

Jailbreak

After nineteen months, Jake was getting out. We were in Texas, and it was August, and you just wanted to kill yourself it was so freaking hot. I put on Jake's favorite sundress, the yellow one with patterned daisies so tiny you had to put your face up close to see them. I'd worn that dress so many times, visiting Jake.

Our Ford Escort was in sorry shape, but it could make it to the jail and back home. I set out to get him alone. I asked Jake if he didn't want Fritz to come along, but he said no, Fritz could come over later, after he and I had spent the day together.

When I got to the jail I went through security and signed a bunch of papers. It would be the last time I'd have to be there, which should have made me nothing but happy, but it also felt strange. The guard stood and hiked his pants up, making the gun in his holster jiggle a little. It sent chills down my spine, the whole place did, always had. He motioned with his head for me to follow him. My sandals clicked as I walked down the hallway to the room where Jake was waiting. This time there would be no physical barrier between us. We could touch each other. I wanted to, but I was scared. We hadn't even kissed for almost two years, but during that time we'd crossed bigger lines than that. Jake, with his words and ideas and instructions. Oh, I liked it all right. But what now?

Jake looked different without the partition in the way. He was wearing his own clothes that I'd brought for the occasion—cut-off denim shorts and a Cuervo T-shirt—but they didn't fit the same. He'd filled out. He was just bursting with muscle. He smiled at me, his eyes blazing brighter than I'd ever seen them, way brighter even, than when he was on one of his best highs. He didn't need that stuff anymore, he said. I hoped he meant it. I didn't want him landing here again.

I stood numbly by while they finished the paperwork, then we walked out together, side by side, still not touching, through the parking lot, the blacktop so hot it felt soft under my feet, hot as Hades, I thought, and wondered whether a host of flames would just break through the tar and burn us to death right then and there.

Of course it didn't. We just stepped silently, awkwardly, kind of avoiding each other, until we got to the car. I unlocked the door for Jake, and he got in, and I went to the other side and got in, too, and then we looked at each other for awhile, and finally Jake reached out and touched my face, just his rough fingertips on my sweaty cheek, just a little. Too much too fast might have killed us both. "Hattie." He whispered my name, but not to me. It was like he had to tell himself it really was me this time, and not a dream.

I didn't need to convince myself it was real. I knew what was happening. I'd waited for it, too, but not like Jake, not in my fantasies. I didn't ever want anything between us to be pretend, so I didn't let myself do that.

Besides, there was Fritz.

Jake was cradling my cheek now with his whole hand, and tears were streaming down his face. I wiped them away, feeling the stubble he could never really get rid of. The only hairless skin on his body was his bald head.

I felt that dome, moist and smooth and pure, and tugged a little my way. Jake gave in and grabbed me, squeezing so tight I thought I'd lose my breath. His head was buried in my chest and I drew in humid air, hard, then I laughed with joy, and Jake stopped crying and laughed, too, and kissed me in that hard, hungry way of his that I missed so much, and we went home.

⊪

Jake spent a little while looking around the apartment, remembering it. He sat at the checkerboard table in the tiny kitchen, then on the ratty green couch in the living room, staring into the TV screen without ever turning it on. Nothing had changed about the place, I made sure of that. I'd told him it would all be waiting for him, and I meant it.

Not everything was the same, though.

I put it out of my mind. I didn't want to think about that, not now when it was Jake I was finally going to have, his hands, his mouth, his cock.

But Jake wouldn't let it be that way. We went into our bedroom. The shades were drawn, the blue curtains pulled to keep it as dark and cool as possible. The sheets were clean and white and turned down. The bed was waiting for us. Jake sat on it, stroking the covers. "Is this where you fucked Fritz?" he whispered. He was rubbing his side of the bed.

I turned away, even though he wasn't looking at me. "Yes," I answered.

"Where else?"

"In the bathroom." My voice was soft, a barely perceptible rasp. It's not like Jake didn't know about it. It was his idea. He didn't want me lonely and suffering. I told him every detail through the partition. Fritz did, too, when he went to see him. "In the kitchen," I said. "I sucked his cock in the kitchen." I felt the warm blush of shame color my already hot cheeks. My pussy tingled, too.

"Come here, baby," said Jake. I stepped forward and stood before him. He started undoing the buttons of my dress, one at a time, first the very top one. "I've been waiting so long to undress you," he murmured. I smiled, one of those hollow, achy smiles. Five buttons, and he opened the dress, like pulling curtains aside, to see my breasts. They were big and round and waiting to be touched. Jake put his hands close to my hard nipples. I took in a deep breath, letting it out slowly as Jake's fingertips brushed against me. He took my tits in his hands, kneading them, rubbing them, dabbing and pinching. My body shivered all over.

I leaned over, offering my breasts to Jake's mouth. "That's it, baby," he said. "Feed me forever and ever." As he sucked me I sat on his lap, straddling his body, my dress hiked up so my pussy and ass felt the bulge of his rod through his jeans. I pressed down on it, and suddenly I was riding him fast, rubbing my clit along his incredible hardness, my tits bouncing in his face. "Wait, Hattie," he said, but I couldn't. He pushed me off him and I landed with my ass on the floor, my legs still splayed. He was standing, ripping off his belt, getting his cock free. His eyes were on fire, and I knew nothing was going to stop him from fucking me silly, nothing was going to get in the way of this animal fuck that I wanted and needed so desperately, no talk of Fritz or jail or anything else, just Jake's cock pounding me.

It sprang from his boxers like a wild snake. It was bigger than I remembered, and I wondered whether hard labor could make a man's dick grow, too. He got on his knees and gripped my ass cheeks from underneath, pulling me into his cock with one harsh tug. I screamed as he entered me, a long wail of relief.

He fucked me so hard I bounced halfway across the room, the old, worn carpet burning my butt cheeks. I came quickly and he stopped, holding me while I wept in his arms. Even when he was flying, Jake was never so far gone that he forgot I was there. "You know what I want to do?" he whispered.

"What?" I said, kissing his earlobe, tonguing the hollow of his neck.

"Taste you," he said. He started to spread me open again, leaning in with his mouth, but I stopped him.

"No," I said, guiding him onto his back on the floor and climbing over him. "I want to suck you, too." The words were barely out before I started licking his big balls, around and around with my tongue, up his shaft and around the swollen, purple head, dipping the tip in my mouth then letting go, dipping then letting go.

At the other end, I could feel how open his mouth was, smothering my pussy with sweet, wet breath. I stopped teasing and took the whole of his rod into my throat while his tongue entered my tunnel, darting in and out.

We sucked each other until I came again, and he came, and we collapsed on the floor, hugging and happy, my dress tangled around my middle. "Hattie," he said. "I am so glad to be home."

I looked at the bed and the virgin sheets. Jake was looking there, too. "What are you thinking about?" I asked.

When he answered, it was like the soft cooing of a bird. "Fritz."

I shivered and kissed him.

⚬

We showered together, soaping and touching each other, remembering each other's skin, contours, favorite places to feel. Jake's arms and belly were taut now, his thighs like iron. I missed his cushiony ass cheeks. Mine were as springy as ever, just sore from rug burn. Jake noticed as he rubbed suds on them. "Honey," he said. "Bend over and let me see." I did, holding onto the towel bar for traction. Jake kissed my boo boos as cool water ran over us both, then made me jump with a start as his palm landed hard on my ass.

I shrieked and he laughed and spanked me again. I lifted my ass higher for more and got it, along with a good fucking from behind. Jake still knew how to play. I had been afraid he'd lose that in jail.

Afterwards, Jake put his shorts back on and I threw a sun dress over my head, and we went in the kitchen and made sandwiches. At four o'clock the doorbell rang. We looked at each other. "I'll get it," said Jake, standing up and buzzing the downstairs entrance. He opened the door and waited there. In a minute, we heard Fritz's footfalls in the hallway.

I couldn't see him at first, but Jake could. He was smiling and I knew he was glad that Fritz was with us now. It made me want to cry for a second, but when I turned to see them embracing, my heart swelled. "Fritz, man," Jake was whispering. "Goddamn, it's good to see you."

Fritz stepped back, his skinny arms twitching at his side. I could see he felt as nervous as I did. He wiped the sweat from his brow, making his bleached white hair stick up like porcupine quills. Jake went into the living room and sat on the couch, and Fritz followed him. "Get us a couple beers," Jake said as Fritz seated himself in our tattered old recliner.

"We don't have any, honey," I said. Neither Fritz nor I drank, and Jake wasn't supposed to.

Jake laughed, his round face jolly in the late afternoon light. "I was just kidding, baby."

Did they both feel as awkward as I did? I looked at Fritz's fingers tapping on the arm of the recliner like he was playing the piano, and decided that he did, at least. Jake was holding some kind of tension, but he was happy, I could feel it. I snuggled in next to him on the couch and put my hand on his thigh. Jake was looking at Fritz, giving him one of those deep, burning stares of his. I kept stroking his thigh, and he kept looking at Fritz. It was easy to see the bulge growing inside his shorts.

That's when I knew that keeping the apartment the same didn't matter at all.

Everything had changed.

⫸

In the bedroom, Jake turned down the clean, white sheets I'd meant for him and me. "Come here," he whispered. "Get in." I started to climb on the bed but he stopped me, smiling and holding my arm gently. "Take off your clothes, baby."

As I pulled off my dress Jake nodded to Fritz and he stripped down, too. It was hot as hell, but his lanky body was shaking as he stood naked. Whatever he was feeling, horny was right up there on the list. His hard dick jutted out in the slight curve that was so familiar to me now, as familiar as Jake's big, straight, steel rod.

Jake's cock was out of his shorts, too, and he was stroking it, motioning to the bed. I got on it and he looked at Fritz, who climbed over me and started kissing me. I knew Jake wanted to see us do it. Every time I told him the details, he said he'd watch us someday. I didn't know whether I wanted him to or not, but it didn't matter. It was because of Jake, and on his terms, that anything ever happened with me and Fritz.

I'd always kept Jake and Fritz separate in my mind, and I tried to keep them separate now as I closed my eyes and felt Fritz's mouth tonguing mine. It was sweet and gentle, like a little boy's, so very different from Jake's, but just as precious. Fritz played with my nipples, pinching and twisting, making my cunt wet and tingly. I parted my legs instinctively and felt Fritz's long fingers slip past my bush to my clit and lips. I moaned as he fingered me, his mouth kissing my tits now, working its way down to my pussy.

I sighed long and deep when his perky little tongue found my clit, jabbing at it and sucking it. I was about to come and I wanted it—one orgasm was never enough, not with Jake or Fritz, they both knew how to make me come forever. I reached down to grab Fritz's head, his spiky, straggly, impossibly blonde locks, so I could push his face hard into my pussy and come all over it.

There was already a hand there. It made me jump. I opened my eyes at the same time my ass lifted off the bed, right into Fritz's face, and I watched Jake palming Fritz's head, petting it and watching me buck and squeal.

I fell back, panting and pulsing. Fritz turned to look at Jake. They were both deathly silent. The only sound in the room was my fast breathing and the soft knocking the shade made against the window sill when a breeze blew. I forced my breath to slow and settle. Fritz and Jake's faces moved closer to each other. Jake rubbed Fritz's lips and chin, then licked his fingers. He kissed Fritz, and Fritz kissed him back. I was the one being still now. I'd never thought of this. I wasn't a person to think on anything. That was Jake's department.

Fritz pulled away from Jake and scrambled backwards on the bed. He was sitting, his hands on the sheets behind him, his legs bent and propped open, presenting his cock and balls to Jake, who took the invitation.

Jake kneeled and clamped his big, strong hand around Fritz's slender, curved dick, showering the tip with gentle, tiny kisses. His tongue licked Fritz's cockhead like it was candy. That hollow feeling came back to my heart, and I wanted to cry. We never talked about this. As I realized that I became angry. Jake had his whole mouth around Fritz's cock now, and he was sucking it like he knew how.

Rage filled my body like heat at high noon. What the fuck was Jake doing? He looked at me like he heard what I was thinking. His crystal blue eyes were shining, and for a fleeting second I thought he'd found some junk and was tripping, but I knew he wasn't, I knew in my soul that heroin really was in the past. He kept Fritz's cock in one hand, holding my gaze until I understood, and why should I have been surprised. Jerking off could never have kept Jake happy for all that time, any more than it could me.

Fritz was shaking like a leaf now. I don't think I ever saw him so excited. It was kind of humorous, but I kept the laugh to myself and instead just smiled a teary smile at my love. He went back to work on Fritz's cock. It didn't take much. For some reason, Fritz didn't seem to have his usual control.

Jake was the only one of us that hadn't come, and I was glad when he took me in his arms and fucked me, long and slow, clinging hard to my shoulders and crying real tears. When he finished I saw that Fritz had left. "He's gone," I said.

"Mmmm," Jake murmured. "He'll be back."

And we slept.

FLOW

Georgia gave birth in September, and now it was June, and she thought if she didn't get laid soon she'd lose her mind. She loved motherhood, that wasn't the problem, if you could call it a problem. Georgia didn't think of it that way. Her warm tingly insides and the incessant longing she felt were so full of achingly sweet promise, she could hardly think of them as problems. They were delicious, a kind of horny she'd never felt before childbirth, nursing, and parenting a tiny little person.

At nine months old, Devin sat up, crawled, laughed, and babbled the most endearing syllables. She loved his cruising, the way he supported himself on his wobbly but ever stronger legs, then grabbed onto chairs, tables, and whatever else he could find to get from point A to point B. It really kept you on your toes, this mothering thing. Georgia would think she had everything babyproofed, then Devin's chunky little fingers would wrap around the brass pole of a floor lamp and send it crashing to the floor. Georgia vividly remembered the day that happened, and the jolt of fear that coursed through her.

Thankfully nothing broke except the bulb. Devin got scared, too, but his tears were nothing a little nursing couldn't cure.

Ah, nursing. Devin loved it, and so did Georgia. She loved the way his head turned to the side, his mouth opening and closing, searching, then clamping down and sucking hard, swallowing fast to keep up with the steady stream of milk. He had a strong latch, and Georgia was prolific.

Before pregnancy, Georgia thought she'd understood the meaning of the word sensual, but living for nine months with a baby swimming inside her, pushing the baby out and gathering his hot, wet body to her, watching the way he sought her physical presence with unabashed, unashamed, complete enthusiasm—this was sensual in ways she never imagined.

There were difficulties, of course. Engorgement, a cracked nipple, interrupted sleep, spitting up, cutting teeth. Once in a while, Devin would bite, and the quick chomp would give her a sharp, unexpected stab of pain. Although she never encouraged it, and wouldn't say she enjoyed it, the rapid, fleeting hurt ripping through her breast at the same time she was swimming in a warm bath of endorphins wasn't altogether unpleasant.

One delicious day flowed into the next, but it wasn't quite enough. When Devin turned the corner on six months, she started thinking about sex a lot. On the nights she didn't fall asleep as soon as she hit the bed, she masturbated, licking her fingers and dipping them into her wet pussy, wet, wet, everything about her life seemed wet since she'd become a mother. She bought a vibrator and tucked it under the pencils and notepads in her night table drawer. It was purple silicone, and looked alarmingly like one of Devin's baby toys. She tried not to think about that when he took the toy and stuck it in his mouth, but sometimes she had to put him in the playpen her mother had given her that she never used otherwise, and take her vibrator into the bathroom. She wondered what her mother would think if she knew that what she'd really given her daughter was a come break.

It made her laugh, but the vibrator was getting less and less satisfactory. Instead of sating her, it seemed she just got hornier. She wanted a flesh and blood cock, that was all there was to it, so she agreed when her best friend Ruth suggested a blind date with a guy from her office. As it turned out, Georgia wasn't horny enough to fuck just anyone. She didn't like the guy. Finding someone she liked had always been a challenge. She hadn't let it stop her from becoming a mom—sperm banks were available, and she was a successful businesswoman with a home office, so why wait for a marriage that might never happen? She didn't much care for the idea of marriage, anyway, although since she had Devin she understood the appeal of having a partner, both to share the workload and the milestones.

Ruth was the perfect auntie, but she was a busy woman and not around a lot of the time. Instead, Georgia shared her Devin trials and tribulations with Cora, the nanny who came to the house twenty hours a week so Georgia could work. In the end, it was Cora who helped Georgia out of her horny rut.

They were in the living room, and Cora had called Georgia away from her desk to comfort Devin. Cora could be counted on to take care of things and leave Georgia undisturbed, but she wouldn't hesitate to interrupt when Devin really needed her.

"You are bursting," she said as Devin hungrily sucked on one of Georgia's breasts and the other dripped with milk, leaving a dark, wet stain on her T-shirt.

"I know," laughed Georgia. "My cups runneth over." Her letdown had slowed as Devin got older, but it was still there, and while it could be a nuisance, Georgia didn't mind. She liked the tingly, hot feeling it produced, and the responsiveness of her breasts to Devin's suckling, his cries, even just thinking about him. She'd found sometimes that when she masturbated, her letdown started. Thinking of that made her blush. She turned her head to the side to hide it.

"What is it?" Georgia knew Cora couldn't read her mind, but she felt like her ridiculously unsatisfied sex drive was written all over the hot redness on her face. Cora smiled. "What, are you thinking about someone?"

Georgia laughed. "No," she said, relieved to be able to give an honest answer even though Cora had guessed at the truth.

"Hmmm," said Cora, tipping her head to the side and smirking slightly. "What about Andy?"

"Who?"

"Andy. The guy who shoveled your driveway all winter."

Andy had been Georgia's neighbor for almost a year. Georgia hardly noticed him while she was pregnant, and paid him little mind for the first few months of Devin's life. But during the harsh winter, he had demonstrated remarkable chivalry, not to mention physical stamina, clearing her driveway and sidewalk for almost every storm.

Georgia would sleep as late as possible, trying to catch up on rest she'd missed feeding Devin or walking the floor with him, and when she looked outside at the white world her pathways were all clear. If she managed to get up early enough she'd see Andy out there, working, and would find herself watching him until he noticed her, and acknowledged her with a wave and a smile that were so charming and unassuming they might just as well have been a bow.

It did create a slight feeling of helplessness in her which she didn't like, so a couple of times she managed to get herself, then Devin, bundled up, and with his body firmly affixed to the front of hers in the baby carrier, get to the snow before Andy.

A couple of times they encountered each other, and as Georgia thought back to those times she realized that yes, there was something there, why hadn't she figured it out sooner? Was it the freezing cold, the unattractive parkas, or the presence of Devin pressed up against her that rendered her clueless? Or was it that for so long she'd been mostly away from adult company other than Cora, and sometimes Ruth, and occasionally the women she met at the new moms group she joined, and of course her clients. Now that Cora had mentioned Andy, Georgia realized it was a pretty good idea. "Andy." She spoke it aloud.

"Yes, Andy," echoed Cora. "He likes you, clearly."

"I've hardly spoken to him," said Georgia.

Cora put her hands on her hips and raised her eyebrows at Georgia. "You talked to him at the holiday party. Then he spends the whole winter shoveling without being asked. I'd say it's pretty obvious."

Georgia laughed, remembering that encounter. The party was thrown by the townhouse association, and she hadn't wanted to go, but Laura, the chairwoman, called everyone personally, reminding them to bring something for the Yankee Swap.

It had been nice to see some of her neighbors and catch up, and she remembered Laura introducing her to Andy, but at that point Georgia wasn't thinking about much of anything except getting back to Devin.

Andy had worn a green sweater, jeans and boat shoes with no socks. He was holding some kind of gingerbread-y craft beer. Laura was obsessed with craft beer, but Georgia could really care less, she was happy to drink a boring old Heineken, which was thankfully available, since she'd made the decision to allow herself half a bottle.

Not only was Andy's clothing casual, his hair—reddish brown with a serious wave—had a tousled look that suited him well. Despite being clean shaven, his thick eyebrows and square jaw gave him a rugged look that was both enhanced and tempered by a boyish smile.

Laura had stuck around after the introduction, discussing beer varieties. Due to her lack of interest, Georgia didn't participate in the conversation, but she remembered thinking that Andy seemed mildly impatient, looking over at her every so often and smiling a little. She could tell he wanted to talk, but then she started wondering how Devin was doing, and she felt her breasts swell and tingle, and before she knew it milk had seeped right through her bra and onto her red sweater. As she folded her arms over her chest to hide the quickly expanding wet spots and hopefully stay the flow, she noticed Andy glancing at her chest. He looked away immediately, and Georgia tried to turn to Laura to say something about the weather, or the mulled cider, or the cookies, but she was gone.

Georgia shrugged. "My baby's at home," she said.

"I've seen you out walking with him," said Andy. "He's cute."

His use of the male pronoun annoyed Georgia, who figured Andy had no way of knowing if Devin was a boy or a girl. "His name is Devin," she said haughtily.

"I know," said Andy. "Laura told me."

Before Georgia had time to think about that, Devin was there, in Cora's arms, his eyes pleading and his lower lip trembling. "I'm so sorry," Cora was saying, shaking her head.

"Oh, it's fine," said Georgia, mostly relieved.

She'd left, and that was the last time she'd spoken with Andy except for the awkward driveway encounters. Georgia thought it would be pretty easy to remedy that. First, she grilled Cora, who reported that whenever she did laundry on Saturday mornings, she always ran into Andy in the laundry room.

Was he so ordinary, so predictable, as to do his laundry at the same time every week? Then again, a man who could take care of himself, and take care of things like laundry- that was nice. None of this mattered, of course, for her current purposes, but it was her nature to think about such things, which probably had something to do with why she was still single.

Georgia arrived in the laundry room around 9:30 on Saturday morning, and though she hung around reading board books to Devin and playing peek-a-boo and pat-a-cake with him for an hour, Andy didn't show up. She grilled Cora again, who shrugged and pleaded ignorance. She tried again the following week, but didn't strike gold until week three.

The diapers were already in the dryer by the time Andy got there. Georgia was sitting in one of the plastic orange bucket chairs, nursing Devin, who was still wrapped up cozily inside the sling. She'd nodded off, but the sound of a washer door closing jolted her awake.

"I'm so sorry," said Andy. "I was trying to be quiet."

Georgia had been dreaming about a difficult work client, and it took her a minute to get her bearings. She was squinting, groggy, and to top it she could feel a tiny bit of drool on her chin. She didn't dare wipe it away, that would only make things worse. She was trying to figure out how to get out of her predicament without too much embarrassment when Devin did one of his rare chomps. She shrieked, quick and shrill, and the arms that were already around Devin reflexively cradled him tighter. Andy looked confused, and apologetic. "Did I scare you?"

"No, no," said Georgia, shifting in her seat and lifting Devin out of the sling. "It was the baby."

Andy looked unsure of what the baby actually did, which was just as well. Said baby was squirming wildly in Georgia's arms, so she leaned over to put him down and let him crawl around the room to his heart's content. When she stood up she realized she hadn't pulled down her shirt, which might have fallen into place of its own accord if it wasn't prevented from doing so by the sling.

So there it was, her freshly nursed nipple, pink and protruding, its dampness glowing under the harsh laundry room lights. Georgia yanked her shirt down, which made the sling jimmy up over her chin. She got it out of her face and saw that Devin's hands and knees had taken him halfway out the door. She moved to retrieve him, but Andy was there first, scooping him up with a big smile. "Hey, you," he said. "Where do you think you're going?"

Thank goodness for Devin, who'd unwittingly distracted both of them from a disastrously uncomfortable moment. If Andy had seen her bared nipple and general dishevelment, there was no sign of it. He was making faces at Devin and playing with him as though nothing had happened. "He likes you," said Georgia, delighted.

As soon as she said it, Devin's attention switched to Georgia. He got a pouty look on his face and held out his arms in her direction. "Oops," said Andy, "spoke too soon."

"Nah," said Georgia. When Andy passed Devin to her their hands met briefly. The touch reminded her of the reason she was there in the first place, but trying to have a flirty conversation with a man while having your face pawed by a baby wasn't easy. Devin's fingers squeezed her cheeks and slipped inside her mouth every time she tried to speak. Then the dryer buzzed. "Do you mind?" she asked, handing Devin to Andy and leaning over to gather a boatload of hot, dry cotton diapers. She realized if she'd been thinking clearly, she would have come with cute camisoles and sexy lingerie, but the heck with it. She couldn't court the same way she used to, that was just reality.

When she finished she took Devin back and tucked him into the sling. Andy sat down in one of the orange chairs and pulled out a book. It was the last "Harry Potter" book, which made Georgia laugh. "I haven't even read those yet," she said.

"My nephew sent it to me," said Andy. "It's all he talks about so I need to be informed."

"How sweet," said Georgia, thinking it was maybe a little too sweet. Then he smiled wickedly and his eyes locked with hers and said, no, not too sweet, not on your life. The horniness that had been simmering inside her started boiling, realizing, perhaps, it was on the verge of release.

"What are you doing tonight?" asked Georgia. Motherhood seemed to make her more forward and less subtle than she used to be, or maybe she'd just developed a better appreciation for the value of time.

Andy disappointed her by saying, "I have a work party." Georgia supposed it was her cue to ask about his job, but at that moment she couldn't care less. Before she could think of her next move, Andy said, "I'm free right now."

Could she be so rash? Yes, her churning pussy said. Of course. It was a little after noon, close to Devin's naptime. He was already nodding off in her arms, his dear head sinking toward his chin as they spoke. "What about your laundry?" she said, motioning towards the machine. It was only on the first rinse cycle.

He stood up. "I can get that later," he said.

"Okay," she said. "Let's go."

⊕

Andy carried the laundry basket full of diapers back to Georgia's townhouse and set it down near the couch while Georgia carefully took Devin, now fast asleep, out of the sling, and even more carefully laid him down in the empty playpen. He squirmed a little, but it was a contented squirm, punctuated by one of those amazing baby sighs. It was so heartwarming that Georgia almost forgot about Andy's presence in the room. She took the pastel green blanket her mother had crocheted and draped it over Devin. He didn't stir. Playpen, blanket, perfect. Thanks, Mom.

Andy came up next to her and they watched Devin in the playpen. "How long does he sleep?" asked Andy.

The hotness level in the room had gotten so thick Georgia felt like she was swimming in it, every breath increasing the fiery feeling sinking from her belly into her crotch. "It depends," she said, and could hear in her own voice the layers of messages that had nothing to do with Devin's nap. "Sometimes an hour, sometimes more. Sometimes only fifteen minutes."

"Is that all?" said Andy, reaching out to touch her shoulder. "We shouldn't waste any time, then."

Georgia looked at his hand on her shoulder, bare save for the thin, stretchy strap of her camisole and the wider, stretchier strap of her nursing bra. The hand looked strong, but it was touching her with the utmost gentleness, its thumb making almost imperceptible motions near the skin of her collarbone, teasing her. "I've never thanked you properly for all your help this winter," she whispered.

"What help?" he asked, moving closer and slipping his free hand around her waist.

"All that shoveling," she said, returning the hug. She even slipped her hands under his shirt. He felt solid, like he worked out, but his skin was soft. Georgia wanted to fall into it, to lose herself in it, she wanted it badly and she wanted it now, but Andy took a step back, away from her.

For a second she thought something had happened, but Devin was still sleeping soundly, the doorbell hadn't sounded, the phone hadn't buzzed. "That was hard work," he said. "You should thank me properly."

In any other context the words would have been rude, but Georgia understood him completely. She took his hand and led him into the bedroom, then knelt down so her face was level with his jeans, which did little to hide the large hard, bulge of his cock.

"I'll do my best to give you what you deserve," she said, unbuttoning his pants, unzipping, reaching inside. As he rolled down his jeans so they cradled his hips, Georgia successfully got his cock out of his boxers. It sprang at her and she grabbed it with her fist, squeezing and stroking its hot purple goodness. She intended to suck it—god, it had been so long since she did that—but she didn't want just his cock, she wanted his balls, too, and they were still lurking behind the slit of his boxers.

In she reached, and took out his sack, and started there, licking the soft, rugged skin, lifting his balls gently with her tongue then releasing them to droop underneath his rod. She turned her attention there next, giving that as good of a tongue bath as she'd given his balls, working her way along the shaft, the body, and the head, tasting the smidge of salty wetness there. It was delicious, and she opened her mouth to receive his big head, taking it in until it touched the back of her throat.

Andy stroked her hair, softly, then harder, squeezing it in his hands and pulling just enough to make her suck harder and faster. While she did, she ran her tongue along the underside of his dick, and held the base of it hard with her hand. "Suck me," he said. "Do it." She glanced up to see his face but he was looking upward, as though in a rapture. His moans indicated he would come soon, and she wanted him to, she wanted to make him shoot right into her mouth, but he had other ideas.

He pulled her away by the hair, not hard enough to hurt but hard enough for her to feel it. She didn't know she would, but she liked the roughness. She liked it a lot. "Get up," he ordered her, and she sprang to her feet and lifted her arms as he pulled off her shirt. She maneuvered the bra herself so it fell away easily, and he took her milk-filled breasts into his hands and stroked them.

It was the first time her breasts had been touched sexually since they'd taken on their true function, that of feeding another human being. Or was that their true function? This pleasure, this joy, this crazy good feeling that went through her whole body while Andy played with her tits had to be just as much their mission. Her nipples were so much fatter now. He took one between two fingers and squeezed. "My god, that feels amazing," she said, looking down and watching as he leaned over and licked each nipple in turn, one then the other. In the middle of the desire that coursed through her she recognized another feeling, the tingling to life of her milk, the hard pull of it from the back of her breasts into the tunnel of her nipple. She knew it was about to release, she could feel it. She started to push his head away but he'd already taken her right nipple into his mouth and was sucking it. When he realized his mouth was full of milk he pulled away, laughing.

He must have swallowed it, she thought, smiling to herself. Though he'd stopped sucking, her letdown was still in play. White, warm milk dripped onto the floor. She sat on the bed, cupping her breasts with her hands to try and catch the milk. Andy yanked her skirt down, then peeled off the gray lacy panties she'd had to dig to the bottom of her underwear drawer to find. He fingered her pussy, so wet, as wet as her breasts that were now covered with dripping milk. He took her swollen clit between two fingers and squeezed it the way he'd squeezed her nipples, then thrust a finger up her cunt so hard it made her yelp. After about three seconds of finger fucking and clit rubbing, she came, hard and loud. The moan that came out of her was long and soulful.

She looked through the open doorway, but Devin showed no signs of stirring. Georgia stayed splayed while Andy dug through the pocket of his blue jeans, looking for something. He pulled out a condom, rolled it onto his protruding cock, and asked Georgia if she wanted to be fucked.

"Yes," she said, propping herself up on her elbows and leaving her legs open. Really, she thought she'd never wanted to be fucked so much in her life.

Andy grabbed her by the buttocks, lifting her hips so he could thrust deep into her, but instead of doing that he just teased her hole with the tip of his dick. It was exquisite torture, feeling the hot head dancing around her clit and lips. "Tell me," he said. "Tell me to do it."

Georgia said, "Fuck me." She looked at his long, thick cock playing with her pussy. She wanted to see it slide inside her, little by little, then fuck her hard. "Put your cock in me."

He obeyed, slipping inside her slowly. He put her hips down and Georgia grabbed her legs under the knees to open them as far as they would go. They both watched Andy's cock fill up her pussy, then pull out and do it again. With every thrust Andy moved a little bit faster, and after every few he grabbed onto his dick and rubbed the head of it around her clit, which was building its way to another orgasm. "Will you come again?" Andy asked as he fucked her.

Georgia responded with an affirmative moan, and Andy withdrew. He got down on his knees and covered her pussy with his mouth, licking her lips, fucking her with his tongue. When he drew her nub into his mouth and sucked it she exploded again, and he held his mouth against her pussy for a second while it gushed and throbbed.

Then he stood up and pulled her up by the hand, grabbed her hips and one shoulder from behind and gently pushed them forward. She understood immediately and got down on her hands and knees, opening her legs just in time to receive his cock again. There was no slowness about this fuck. Her whole body bounced, and she held onto the edge of the bed as he pumped her, slapping her ass cheeks, making the skin there burn and sting while her insides were penetrated with delicious, hot hardness.

When he came he grabbed onto her ass and squeezed and bucked and let out a long, slow hiss that sounded like air being released from a balloon. He pulled out and knelt down to hug her. She turned to face him and return the hug, and he kissed her softly, and she realized it was their first kiss. She savored it; motherhood had made her so much better at savoring things.

Andy laid his head on her shoulder and she peered through the doorway, where she could just see the lump Devin's blanket-covered feet made. It was still, but the sight and thought of him called forth her milk again. She felt the rumble deep inside her breasts, the release at her nipple, the warm dripping, the wetness landing on her skin and Andy's. He didn't move, just held her tighter. She echoed his stillness, and let the flow happen.

Training

Except for masturbating, I had always been a good girl, until the day Audrey ate me out in the bathroom at work.

We worked for men, in a law office. They had their own bathroom down the hall. Ours was closer to the work area, a big room with only one toilet, no stalls. I always hated that I had to piss with my boss sitting on the other side of the wall.

When Audrey walked into the bathroom she found me sitting on the closed toilet seat, crying. Nothing in particular had happened to cause this. Crying in the bathroom at work was my way of letting off steam, and it was Friday, 6:20 p.m., and everyone else had gone home, and I was tired, and I had nothing to do for the weekend but read magazines and landscape the yard.

Audrey was new. She'd replaced a partner's secretary a week before, and I had been training her, revealing the particulars of the office machinery, the daily routines, the quirks of the lawyers, how they liked their letters typed, how they wanted their phones answered.

Now, at 6:20 p.m. on Friday, Audrey was done being initiated, and I found myself feeling a little sad. I hated training new people, but Audrey had been fun. She didn't have that angry hiss beneath the smiling veneer like most of the secretaries that came through the office. Audrey seemed happy to be servile to her lawyer, and to me, too.

By noon on Monday, she'd learned how I take my coffee, and started delivering it to me every day. By Tuesday, she found the spot on my shoulder that typing and gardening always tightened. On Wednesday, she placed a vase holding a pink, budding tulip on my desk. Thursday she took me to lunch at a vegetarian restaurant, and spent a long time eating an artichoke, carefully peeling away each individual skin and sucking out the meat and juices before descending reverently on the heart. By that time, I was pretty sure she liked me, and I thought I liked her, too, whatever that meant.

Then came Friday, and the bathroom.

I heard the door open and looked away from the dark wet spots my tears made on the terra cotta floor tiles, up at Audrey's cheerful, generous form. She stood next to me, one hand resting lightly on the white edge of the sink, the other at her cheek, fingers lightly curved, absently tapping near the corner of her lips, no lipstick, but red anyway. They were curled into the suggestion of a smile, a new idea forming, or an old one, coming forth. The word "Ellen" left her mouth like a breath, not spoken, not whispered; involuntary, but with intent.

For the first time I let my eyes fall directly where my peripheral vision had been all week, onto Audrey's body, her gloriously large breasts, pushed up under her soft v-neck sweater so a long line of cleavage poked through. I imagined the creamy, moist darkness of that slit, and my pussy throbbed in ways it only did when I flicked on my vibrator.

Before I had time to pull back from that feeling, Audrey was kneeling in front of me, clean white fingertips taking the tears from my face with almost touches, licking the salt from her hands, smiling bigger until I felt my own face crack into a grin, begin to laugh, make other sounds of glee and awe as Audrey reached for my tweed skirt, pinching my nipples on the way down. She grabbed the elastic waist of the skirt and my panty hose, pulling them down, taking my underwear with them, all the way to my flat brown shoes, slipping everything off and leaving it in a pile.

Audrey slid her palms between my thighs and gently pushed out until I felt the warm air of the room brush my bare cunt, which Audrey was looking at with admiration, her face coming closer until I could only see the top of her head, the gleaming reddish black hair, and I thought how all week I had been watching the way it moved and fell and tickled the tender skin of her neck.

The tip of Audrey's nose nuzzled me. She giggled into my pussy, and the breath and vibration made me shudder. I opened my legs wider, one foot on the wall, the other on the sink where Audrey's hand had been.

Audrey began licking my pussy, mixing wet with wet, more wet warm liquid collecting in delicious swelling swirls, her finger inside me, moving in and out, then making a hook, rubbing and caressing at intolerably pleasurable places, sucking and rubbing until I exploded into her mouth.

I let gravity take me slowly downward, sliding off the closed toilet seat until I was kneeling on the tiles. I nudged Audrey until she leaned against the wall of the bathroom, and I buried my head in her sweaty, dark cleavage.

I rested there until my tongue started to move and find new places to go, places where I'd never been, but no matter.

I had been training women for so long. I knew everything I needed to know.

consuela

We courted over a checkerboard table for two, Consuela and I, she licking the brown head of her chocolate cone, me slurping the pure white of my cherry vanilla, plucking out the fruity, burgundy nuggets with my teeth.

Our class had been meeting since the semester began in cold, snowy January. It wasn't until March that I noticed Consuela watching me from across the lecture hall, her dark eyes peering through the flutter of her lashes, her face shrouded by long hair, falling like black silk curtains around her head.

At first I caught her in my peripheral vision, and I'd only peek back when I knew she wasn't looking, like when she was frantically scribbling notes, or walking out of the room, her round ass resplendent in red corduroys. But after awhile I got bolder and met her eyes. She'd stay perfectly still, just cock her lips sideways in a lopsided almost smile, and her eyes would change, the irises turning darker and shinier somehow, flaring as if lit from within.

We played like that for weeks, until she was winking at me and blowing kisses. All I could do was smile in return, but my smile must have told her how much I wanted it. What I wanted specifically, I had no idea. I'd never made it with a woman before, hadn't even thought about it except briefly when a former boyfriend wanted to have a threesome. I'd said no, and moved on to the next boring guy. But Consuela wasn't boring, and I found myself fantasizing about her, perusing the internet for pictures of women doing it, looking for information on how to eat pussy, fist, all that stuff I thought lesbians did.

By the time Consuela walked up to me after class, actually spoke to me for the first time ever, just thinking about her made me wet. Looking at her made me throb. Having her stand in front of me and actually say something was unbearable.

It was May, and we were getting ready for finals. "Hey," she said, tossing her mane behind her shoulder, sleek olive skin peeking out of the edge of her blue tank top. "Let's go out."

"Now?"

"Yeah," she said. "Let's go." I followed her like a puppy dog. Consuela liked to be in charge. It was to be the basis for our relationship, and something that elicited the most excruciatingly wonderful orgasms I'd ever had.

That warm day in May, Consuela led me to the ice cream shop, where she ordered a chocolate cone for herself and a cherry vanilla one for me. She carried both to a table and nodded at the chair I was to use. I parked my hot ass down, and watched Consuela take the seat across from me. When she handed me the cone, I was salivating.

I held it, waiting for her to tell me what to do. I was already with the program, without even knowing what the hell the program was. Consuela told me later I was a natural, whispered it wet into my ear, biting vigorously on my earlobe, after fucking my brains out with the biggest dildo she could find.

She rolled out her tongue first, showing it to me. It was long and pink, and curled at the tip. She brought the cold, wet ice cream to bear on the length of it, licking over and over, never taking her eyes off me.

Once she had the cone good and licked, she reached across the table and shoved it in my mouth, hard, so that I had to bite it to keep it from choking me. I laughed into the ice cream. I was loving it, even the shock of cold in my mouth and the pain in my teeth.

We went to the ice cream parlor after class for the next three weeks. I practiced every technique I could on those ice cream cones, getting ready. A lot of it I copied from Consuela.

On the fourth week, after final exams, Consuela's bare foot found my pussy under the table. I was wearing a sundress with no underwear, per Consuela's instructions. The ball of her foot sank into the warm wet of my cunt, rubbing. I closed my eyes and tried not to moan.

"Keep licking," Consuela ordered, and I went back to my ice cream cone, pretending it was Consuela's cunt, sucking and mouthing while her toes tickled my pussy. Her big toe found my hole, and I spread my legs wider to receive it, moving my ass back and forth gently on the chair. She fucked me like that for a minute, then brought her toes up to my clit, pressing hard on it in circular motions. I came in about a second. As I sat at the little checkerboard table panting in ecstasy, Consuela's hand, the one holding her cone, reached underneath and planted the rounded, well-licked, freezing head of chocolate ice cream onto my steaming, juiced pussy.

I cried out so loudly the other people in the shop turned to look. Consuela laughed, and so did I.

It definitely wasn't the last time she surprised me.

❖

I took longer than Consuela did to finish our final exam, but when I left the classroom and entered the hallway, I found her waiting, leaning against the graffiti covered wall with her head tilted to one side and her books hugged to her chest.

She shifted them to the left and made a cradle with her elbow, then curled the index finger of her right hand around a belt loop in my jeans and pulled. She pulled me two blocks off campus, all the way to her apartment, a messy studio on the fourth floor. When we walked into the building she made me go first, and alternated between pushing me up the stairs and squeezing and twisting my butt cheeks.

The door was unlocked. Consuela dropped her books on the counter in the kitchenette. I put mine on a chair, and turned to look at the king size futon on the floor. It was covered with bright red satiny sheets, littered with glittery, sequined pillows of black and royal blue and mustard yellow, fraying tassles hanging from their corners. An upside down wooden crate served as the night table, covered with an embroidered cloth. A glass lamp was on it, surrounded by lord knows how many harnesses tangled up with each other, two tubes and one bottle of lube, and some other things I couldn't identify.

Consuela went into the kitchenette and lifted something out of a pot on the stove. When she turned around, I saw that it was a jet black dildo, a slightly curved, thick cock with a generous head. She smiled at me and kissed the head, then pointed to the bed. "Get on it," she said. "On your knees." I took off my sandals and went to the middle of the futon, which was much cushier than I expected it to be. I was wearing dungaree shorts, and the satin felt smooth and luxurious under my bare knees. "Watch me," said Consuela. "Don't take your eyes off me."

She put the base of the dildo between her teeth and held it there, sticking out of her mouth, while she pulled down each strap of her tank dress until it was hanging on her like a skirt. Her breasts were big and firm, round like the rest of her, the nipples as hard and erect as the cock in her mouth. She wiggled her hips until the dress fell in a pile at her feet, and I saw that she was already wearing a harness, a black leather one wrapped around her hips, just underneath the luscious mound of her belly, her bush as shiny and black as her hair. It became the black cock's bush as she took it out of her mouth and strapped it on.

She laughed and thrust it back and forth at me a few times, then said, "Strip, Kathy."

I undid my shorts, pulled them off, and lifted my shirt over my head. I was in such a tizzy it got stuck around my neck, and I fiddled with it frantically for a few seconds before getting it all the way off. I was naked on my knees in front of Consuela now, and she was coming toward me, her gorgeous lips that I hadn't yet kissed, her delicious tits that I wanted to suck, her big black cock that was going to have its way with me. Somewhere underneath it all was the pussy I had been imagining.

As she walked towards me, slow, her hand wrapped around the dildo, fondling it, I thought about how I looked to her. I was nothing special. Where she had long, black, phenomenal hair, mine was mousy brown, short enough to show off the multiple piercings along the edges of my ears. Where her body was voluptuous and sensual and sexy, mine was thin and angular, with small boobs, the kind people like to refer to as perky.

My nipples were pink, though, and I found out later Consuela liked that, the way she liked my boniness, my pale skin, and especially my lack of pussy hair, which I'd been shaving since I discovered how much better cocks and tongues and fingers felt without it.

Consuela kept coming at me until the dildo was hitting me in the face. She whapped one cheek, then the other, then pushed me over with her knees. I lay on my back, my legs outspread, my mouth and my pussy watering. She put one foot on my belly, then reached over me to grab a pair of black leather studded bracelets held together by a silver chain.

Once she had them she knelt over me, the cock resting happily in the space between my tits, and grabbed my hands, putting one bracelet on, then the other. Once I was good and cuffed, I lay back, stretching my arms over my head and my legs out long and wide. Consuela whispered in my ear. "Are you ready for Mama?" she asked.

"Mmmmm," I murmured, completely psyched about the luxury of being helplessly fucked.

"Mama's going to take care of you," Consuela whispered, licking my ear, running her tongue along the studs and hoops. She licked along my cheek, to my mouth, her fleshy, tawny lips opening my thinner, pinker ones, kissing me long and deep, fucking my mouth with her tongue. I started to tongue her back, but she pulled away and smacked my face. "Bad girl," she said. "Don't do that without permission." I smiled and she smacked me again. Her tits were hanging low, dangling against my chin, driving me nuts. "Tell Mama you're sorry."

"I'm sorry, Mama," I said, restraining myself from lifting my head and trying to nibble on one of her tits.

"That's a good girl," said Consuela, taking my nipples between her fingers, pinching and twisting. I moaned and she did it harder. "Does it hurt?" she asked.

"Yes," I whispered.

"Does it hurt good?"

"It hurts fucking great," I said, and moaned louder as she started sucking my nipples, nursing them with her teeth and lips and tongue until my whole body was hot and buzzing. She put her hand around my pussy, tickling my lips and clit with her long red fingernails. I moved my hips up and down, opened my legs wider, lifted my ass to open my cunt as far as it would go. She licked the smooth skin around my clit and lips, around and around until I thought I'd die from anticipation. Then the darting tip of her tongue went inside me, slithering along the inside of my pussy, then out to the lips, sucking one then the other, then my clit, until I came in her open mouth.

She stayed there for a minute, letting my cunt throb, then she got back on her knees and grabbed a tube of lube. She juiced up the dildo and knelt between my legs, grabbing my hips hard and pulling my ass and pussy off the bed and into her, into the black cock, thrusting so deeply I could feel it all the way to my belly. She fucked me hard for a long time, bouncing me against her so fast I could feel my tits shake wildly. My first time with a woman, and I was getting fucked with a cock. It had been a long time before Consuela since I'd gotten anything, but this was definitely different than a flesh and blood dick. Consuela held my hips hard, her eyes rolled back in her head, lovely. It occurred to me that the dick was fucking her, too, that we were connected by it, that it was pleasuring both of us, an instrument of our mutual desire, the energy of our wanting fueling it, making it alive.

Consuela didn't cry out, but I saw her shudder, her body shaking inwardly into orgasm, and my heart melted. Then she turned me over, grabbing my ass cheeks in her fists, slapping them with her hands while she pumped me from behind.

After she finished fucking she ate me again until I came continuously, a cascade of orgasms spilling into her mouth.

Then she lay beside me quietly, stroking my tits and my belly and my bald pussy gently for a few minutes, sighing every so often, smiling. Within that calm, she unbuckled her harness, tossed it and the dick aside, freed me from the cuffs, and hugged me close. Her soft, round body felt heavenly pressed up against me, her tits mashed against mine, her silky bush on my bareness down there. She started kissing me again, and put one of my hands on her breast. I squeezed it and played with it just the way I wanted to. I knew she wasn't Mama now, just Consuela, the hot, lovely, Consuela I'd been imagining for so long.

I took her breasts in my mouth, back and forth, one to the other, my darting tongue meeting the tip of her hard nipples, my lips covering them, tightening and sucking. My hand played with her pussy all the while, exploring the big lips, tugging at them, fingers pulling back the shaft of her clit to tap on the head, slipping inside to map the inner terrain, finding the good spots that made her scream and pull my hair, her pussy spouting warm and clear.

After that I laid her down on the red satin, among all the wet spots my come and hers had made, and spread her open to see her luscious pussy, brown along the edges, shining and pink and swollen inside, and I ate her like a cherry vanilla ice cream cone, until every drop was finished.

⊕

The semester was over. I had a summer job interning at a newspaper. Consuela was working for a congressional candidate. We met for lunch, chatted about our work, our majors, our childhoods. Nights we spent on red satin, fucking.

After two weeks of heaven, Consuela told me about Leif. "Leif's coming home tomorrow," she said.

"Who's Leif?" I asked sleepily, twirling the soft coils of her bush around my fingers.

"My boyfriend. He's been away, studying overseas. He's coming back tomorrow."

I was only in a little bit of shock. "What does that mean?" I asked.

"Don't worry, Kathy," she whispered, reaching for the cuffs. "You're going to love him."

⊰

Leif arrived in town on a Tuesday. Consuela informed me that she'd need time with him alone, and she'd call me when she was ready for us to meet. I protested, not sure I could bear being without her for very long. She agreed to have lunch with me on Thursday.

We met at a deli, where Consuela ordered an egg salad plate, and I had a reuben with fries. After proceeding through the line, grabbing Diet Cokes and napkins and silverware, we picked a corner table and sat down with our food.

"How's work?" asked Consuela.

"Fine," I said. "The tax override was voted down. That's what I wrote about today."

"Sounds thrilling," said Consuela. "I, on the other hand, went to a dinner with important people last night."

"What did you wear?" I teased, running my toes along her shin, feeling happy and warm.

"Red, of course," said Consuela. "Leif's favorite." I froze and took a deep breath.

Consuela put her hand on mine. "You mustn't be jealous, Kathy. I love you both."

"Then why aren't you seeing me?"

She laughed. "You're a hungry, naughty girl, Kathy." Consuela chewed on a piece of celery. "Friday. We'll go out to dinner."

"You and me?" I asked, favoring denial over reality.

"And Leif," said Consuela. "We'll meet on neutral ground. We'll see how it goes, and take it from there."

"Okay," I said, even though it didn't feel one bit okay.

But at that point, I'd have done anything for Consuela.

⊪

She picked Italian, and I ordered lasagna to avoid the awkwardness of spaghetti or fettuccini. It didn't work, entirely. There was a side of pasta, a pile of smooth noodles covered by shimmering red sauce and salty cheese.

Consuela had no inhibitions about spaghetti or anything else. She ordered Fettuccini Alfredo, and ate it one noodle at a time, just barely using her fork, mostly using her mouth like a vacuum cleaner. She was remarkable, doing it without any noise and with total finesse.

I found myself watching her in between bites of lasagna, enjoying the white sauce that inevitably spilled onto and around her lips, the way she licked it clean with her tongue.

I was also avoiding Leif, who turned out to be the quiet, intellectual type, nothing like I'd imagined.

Yes, I had tried to imagine him. For the painful days without Consuela, I tried to think about what I knew she was planning. What was it about a three way that terrified me? I didn't know, only knew that I would do it if Consuela wanted me to.

"Talk to her, Leif," said Consuela, rubbing the taut muscle on his forearm.

He smiled mildly, showing off his straight teeth, sipping from his cup of tea. "Yes, love," he said with the slightest hint of an accent. "Of course we'll talk." He turned to me. "Kathy, I'm afraid we're both shy."

"She's not shy," Consuela said, and I blushed.

I forced myself to talk. "So you're in law school?"

He shifted in his seat, making himself that much closer to me. "Yes," he said. He'd been drinking dark German beer all night, and I could smell the way it lingered on his breath. It turned me on for a fleeting second and I laughed. I hated a drunk, but I'd forgotten how much I liked the way alcohol made a man's mouth taste.

He smiled as though he knew I wasn't laughing about his choice of career at all, as though he understood. It made me like him a little, although later I figured that his understanding had to do with past experience with that kind of situation, not with me.

I sipped my drink. It warmed my belly, making me relax, and laugh, and sink lower in my seat as Consuela took over the chatting. She was remarkably generous, lavishing attention on Leif and me virtually equally, which made me relax even more. I started to really look at Leif, listen to his deep, resonant voice speak in measured, calm tones. He was extremely mellow, highly articulate, and obviously intelligent. I checked out his hands, large and sinewy, with long, graceful fingers and rounded fingertips. Broad shoulders. Strong. No hair peeking from the open top buttons of his preppy button down shirt. I guessed he was smooth, and perfect, like a marble statue.

After dinner we walked to the Common, sitting on one park bench after another, taking turns being in the middle. Consuela took the first turn, putting her arms around both of us, pulling us in. The park was dark and quiet, the moonlight mixing with the occasional lamp post, glowing in the summer night. She kissed me first, and I rejoiced inside. Then she kissed Leif, put one hand behind my head, and the other behind Leif's, drawing the two heads together, mine and Leif's, until his barely scented beer breath met mine, bitter with Campari, sour with lime, sweet with gelato, and we kissed, our lips finding each other slowly, tentatively, licking and sucking with our teeth and tongues, while Consuela watched, sighing deeply. Her hand stroked my hair as I kissed Leif, enjoying his mouth immensely, but hanging onto her every second, giving myself to her through him.

By the time we hit the fourth bench, we were all kissing at the same time, and finding each other's erect nipples, hard cock, swollen pussies through our clothes, and Consuela said, "Let's go." And of course, I did.

⊹

We went to Leif's, a luxury two-bedroom apartment in a downtown high rise. We were all over each other in the elevator, the whole way up to the twenty-first floor, Consuela pulling up my T-shirt and sucking my breasts, me fondling her pussy under her dress, Leif slipping a hand inside the back of my jean shorts and squeezing my cheeks.

Leif's place was spotless. Clean, orderly, comforting. The kitchen, dining area, and living room were all in one cushy open area, with two more rooms down a small hallway. One was Leif's office, the other the bedroom. That's where we went.

Leif pulled back the spread on the king size bed, covered with clean cotton sheets. Outside the huge picture window, city lights twinkled. I walked up to the sheet of glass, stared into the view, Consuela behind me, pulling off my shorts and shirt. As I looked into the night, watched it unfold far into the distance, I felt like we were flying above the whole world.

When I turned around Consuela and Leif were already naked. He was as well put together as his home, as clean, as inviting, and, as I'd guessed, as perfect. His cock stood straight up, the head peeking out of his foreskin, and I felt a thrill seeing him uncut. He was watching me, too, and I felt a stab of self-consciousness, comparing myself with Consuela's earthy beauty. But he was smiling, a different kind of smile than he'd used in the restaurant, where he'd been all civilized and reserved.

"On the bed, Kathy," said Consuela. "With your back against the headboard." I climbed on the mattress, leaned against the oak headboard, opened my legs to show them both my pussy. Consuela had Leif's cock in her hand, moving back and forth so his dick fully emerged from the foreskin. She was whispering in his ear, mumblings I couldn't understand. Inside I had a vague feeling of not liking that, but I ignored it, transfixed by the sight of Consuela pleasuring Leif with her hand, kissing his mouth and his ear. Despite any jealousy I might have felt, it was a beautiful sight, watching the woman I'd fallen so hard for with a man I knew she loved.

She let go of his cock and led him to the bed where I was waiting. She gently placed him in a kneeling position on the floor, so he was at eye level with my pussy, then put my hand in Leif's hand and climbed onto the bed, leaning her face into my cunt, licking and sucking all the ways she knew I liked. I opened as wide as I could, but I never felt like I could make myself as open as I wanted to be, open enough for Consuela to fall inside me. Leif's hand squeezed mine and I squeezed back as Consuela's mouth took me in. With his other hand he stroked Consuela's gorgeous hair, and whispered, "Yes, love, that's right love, that's beautiful, love." His words echoed in my head—yes, love, good, beautiful, now—until my body shook and pulsed and I lay back, spent and happy.

Consuela knelt beside Leif and kissed him deeply, and the sight of her giving my taste to his mouth both shocked and excited me. After a moment Leif stood up and Consuela slapped his ass. "Go," she said, like she was desperate, like she had been waiting a long time for this moment of watching Leif fuck me.

He took me the way she had the first time, pulling me up by the hips and thrusting hard and deep. The feeling was as new as Consuela's dildo had been—Leif's foreskin, the way it slid along his dick and inside me. Consuela pulled a dildo out of her bag and fucked herself while we fucked. Leif watched her jerking up and down on the dildo until she came, crying out louder than I'd ever heard her. Then Leif pulled out of me and stood on the floor in front of Consuela, taking her by the hair, pulling her head toward him so she could take him in her mouth.

I watched her lick my juices off his hard cock, take the whole length of it in and out, suck it while she worked the base with her hands, until his ass and hips stiffened and he came, Consuela's mouth holding the whole of him until he finished.

They both climbed in bed with me, and we cuddled, Leif and I, with Consuela in between us.

ⵞ

W̲e̲ fell asleep like that.

When I woke the clock said 3 a.m., and Consuela and Leif were still slumbering. She had turned from me toward him, wrapped around him from behind, spoon style. Curled up like that, they looked like two innocent children, and I felt a moment of pure affection before the stronger feelings of anger and jealousy welled up.

Why wouldn't she turn to him instead of me? In all the weeks together, all the intimacy, all the desperate, amazing fucking, we had never actually slept together. She never invited me to stay. I felt furious and vulnerable at the same time.

Leif stirred and opened his eyes, as though awakened by the strength of my emotions. I was lying on my side, propped up on my elbows, and he was looking right at me. He smiled dreamily and, I thought, secretly. "Hi, Kathy," he whispered. This private moment between us surprised me. I found myself blushing and tongue-tied. I liked him.

Before I could begin to process that thought, Consuela woke up, kissing Leif, taking his half-limp cock in her hand and working it. I climbed over her and Leif, so that Leif was in the middle now, and joined her in kissing him, our mouths all meeting and giving, the way they had on the park bench hours before.

I kissed Leif's neck, his nipples, licking and sucking them the way I did to Consuela. While I was doing that, I glanced down at his cock, completely rigid now, Consuela's hand pumping it. The urge to suck dick overcame me. I brought my head close to Leif's hard-on, his knees bent, legs propped open lazily, wanting nothing but to lick him, to love his cock with my mouth.

Consuela's hand grabbing my hair harder than she ever had, jerking my head back until my neck hurt, shocked me. "No," she yelled. "You are not allowed to do that." She was still hold-ing my hair and pulling it. I fought her, thinking this was just part of the game. She slapped my face until it stung.

"Fuck you," I whispered limply. I was crying.

Leif reached his hand to my cheek and wiped a tear with his thumb. "Consuela," he said, like a disapproving father.

"She doesn't get that, and you know it."

"You don't need to be so vicious." Leif's voice was like honey, kind and reassuring. Consuela didn't think so. She sat up in bed, hugging her knees, burying her face in them, her body shaking. Leif took her in his arms to comfort her. "Come on, love," he said, stroking her hair. She embraced him, her face in his chest.

I watched her cry in his arms.

While he kissed Consuela's hair, he glanced up at me and smiled. I thought he wanted to say something, but I couldn't tell what, or maybe I didn't want to know.

⊕

Consuela should have realized that forbidden fruit had to be plucked. Or else she didn't know me well enough, or hadn't paid enough attention, to notice my firmly entrenched rebellious streak. Yeah, I'd play along, I'd be submissive, but don't tell me I can't have something I want, especially if you get it.

I tried to talk to her about it. Why, I asked? Why can I fuck him and touch him and not suck him?

We were in the ice cream parlor, but it wasn't the same. She didn't even order for me, so I ordered for myself. Pistachio, my favorite flavor, but Consuela wouldn't know anything about that. "Because he's my boyfriend," she said. "*My* boyfriend."

"And what am I?"

Consuela blushed, realizing her blunder. "You're my lover." She nudged me under the table with her knee. "I love you."

I looked away. Consuela's hands disappeared under the table, found the backs of my knees. "Come here, girl," she said. "Come to Mama." She pulled me forward and reached for me, but my khaki cut-offs were an impossible barrier between her hands and my pussy.

Still, she was turning me on.

"Let's go to my place," she said. "It's been a long time."

It was true. For the past week, since that first night at Leif's, we had done nothing but fuck together. Consuela still used her dildos, but on Leif, not me.

So I was mad at her, a little. But I wasn't about to say no to having her to myself.

From then on, she made sure we had some Mama time, just me and her, at least on a weekly basis, and sometimes more.

I stopped bugging her, so I'm sure she thought it was taking care of everything.

But there was a lot she didn't know.

⊪

The three of us usually met for dinner, taking turns picking the restaurant. We did that at least three nights during the work week, and we spent every minute of every weekend at Leif's apartment, rolling and fucking in his bed, on his bedroom floor, and in his jacuzzi. We ordered take out and ate it off each other's naked bodies, tits and Thai peanut sauce, ass cheeks slathered with custard, pussies and chocolate mousse. Nothing on Leif's cock, ever. Consuela was getting skittish about flaunting her ownership of Leif's dick, though she sucked it plenty. She seemed guilty afterwards, as if she were worried about me. Even in our private sessions, she was less and less the dominatrix. More and more she'd ask me what I liked, what I wanted. My answers never satisfied her. She kept looking for more, which was fine with me.

Maybe she knew, somewhere inside, what Leif and I were up to. I didn't plan to pursue him, but he came after me, in his classy, understated Leif way, and I went along.

It started with stolen looks and smiles when the three of us were together and Consuela wasn't looking. I tried not to read into those, but meanwhile I fantasized about Leif, not only about sucking his cock, but having him all to myself, which Consuela had made clear was another big no no. It got me remembering how much I liked guys, and reminded me that I had always been straight until I met Consuela. What would I call myself now? Bi? I couldn't imagine myself attracted to another woman as long as Consuela was around. She was definitely all the pussy I needed. But what we were doing was nothing like what I thought lesbians did. All that fisting research had been useless. It was about tits and eating pussy, yes, but mostly it was still about dicks, and as it turned out, I liked that.

I liked Leif's dick, too, more and more. So when he was sneaking private looks at me behind Consuela's back, making eyes in his subtle, obtuse, but highly compelling way, I did it back.

Then he started showing up early for dinner, giving us minutes here and there to talk. "How long have you been with Consuela?" I asked him. I had already asked her, but she said it was none of my business.

"Years," he said. "We met when we were thirteen."

This was shocking news, and made me feel suddenly and woefully insignificant. "How many other toys have you played with?"

I must have sounded angry, because Leif lowered his voice and said, "Do you think I don't care about you, Kathy?"

I loved the way he made it about himself, saying "I" instead of "we."

That night when Leif kissed me, I thought I could forget that Consuela was even there.

❖

In our brief, incomplete conversations, strung together like random, unconnected dots on a page, I learned that Leif had been born abroad, that he'd moved to the States when he was ten, and that he'd felt lost here until he met Consuela, who was also born in a foreign country, and who, according to Leif, decided to keep him. "It's not that I don't love her," he said. "But she doesn't own me, and she doesn't understand that."

Suddenly I was empathizing, thinking, yeah, I know exactly what you're talking about. How long had it been—only a month—since all I wanted was to follow her, to belong to her, to be her little girl. That was forgotten now, end of July, approaching the dog days of August. I found myself thinking desperately about what was going to happen in the fall, when we all went back to school. Working at the newspaper I could do, I could handle that and this new joyous life I'd found. But classes? I pushed the thoughts away. Still, they were there inside me, and like an undiagnosed illness, they did damage.

One night Leif asked me to come to his office after hours. "What about Consuela?" I asked.

"Tell her you're busy," he said.

"She knows I'm never busy," I answered.

"Monday night," he said. "At nine."

So I told Consuela I'd started dating the guy at the newspaper who'd asked me out. That was fine with Consuela. She wanted me to go out with someone, to ease her guilt, I think, which I had admittedly tried to fuel. Every so often I brought up Leif, making pitiful comments about how nice it would be to have him the way she did. Mostly she got pissed off and spat things like, "Find your own cock, Kathy," but I could tell it was getting to her.

Leif's law office was in a renovated historical building downtown. With its ornate wood carvings, it held the authority and command of history. I knocked twice, lightly, and Leif let me into the office, all plush burgundy velvet, sprawling desks, brass lamps.

"Hey," he said, smiling.

"Hey," I answered, following him through the waiting area into a more private area. "Is this your office?" I asked.

"No," he laughed. "Give me a few years." He sat in a black leather chair, looking me in the eye, letting me know what we were there for. He swiveled the chair so it faced sideways and gestured for me to come closer.

I stood in front of him and he hugged me to him, his face buried in my belly, breathing hot through the fabric of my cotton sundress. He turned his face up to look at me. "I want to do everything with you," he said, fingering my belly button through my dress. "I want to kiss you and lick you and fuck you from every direction, and more."

"What more?" I asked, already knowing the answer.

He gently pressed my hips downward. I took the signal and got on my knees, unbuckled his belt, undid his suit pants, and pulled them and his underwear down to his ankles. He played with my hair and I took his hard cock in my hand, pulling back the foreskin to reveal the shining, purple head. The knowledge that I was about to put it in my mouth, taste it, lick it, suck it, was too good to let go of right away.

In the lamplight I stroked it, examined it, studied it all the way from the drooping, loose balls to the head. I had never been allowed to get this close before, to learn all the little details and idiosyncracies of Leif's cock. I saw the deeply patterned ridges of his scrotum, veins running along his rod like roads on a map, the open slit at the very tip. At the sight of the clear fluid oozing from it, I couldn't wait anymore. I licked it off, running my tongue around the incredibly silky skin of his head, along the taut shaft, around the dampness of his balls.

Then I took him full in my mouth, sucking the way I had been longing to, taking his dick into the back of my throat, holding the base and pumping with my hand and mouth at the same time. When I thought he was about to come, I pulled away and licked his inner thighs and his groin, until he was begging me to take him in my mouth again. I kept him going for a long time that way.

While I worked at his dick I found my pussy with my other hand, and let him watch me play with myself whenever I stopped sucking.

Eventually, when we were both good and ready, I kept my mouth on him and let him shoot all the cream he had down my throat, while I rubbed my clit hard enough to come with him.

We stayed in that office for hours, kissing, sucking, fucking.

⅊

Consuela wanted to know all about my dates with George. I told her everything, describing the way I kissed him, all the positions we fucked in, and especially, exactly how I sucked his cock. I told her 69 was George's favorite. As a matter of fact, Leif and I had discovered that 69 suited us better than anything else.

When I talked about it, demonstrating my technique on Consuela's fingers, one at a time, I could see her getting turned on and wet. Then she got mad. "Kathy," she said, "It's not fair for you to suck George and not Mama." We were lying on her messy futon, no red satin now, just flowery cotton sheets with holes. She was wearing her big black dildo, the one she used on me the first time. "Come on, girl," she said, pushing my head down.

I didn't exactly want to do it, but I couldn't imagine saying no. I took the dick in my hand and stroked it while I kissed Consuela's belly, her hips, licked the skin all around her harness. When I ran my tongue along the dildo, the first thing I noticed was the taste, like Consuela, and that surprised me. I thought it would taste fake, but once I started licking Consuela's scent off it I got really turned on, and before I knew it I was sucking hard. Consuela moved with me, murmuring and moaning. Her pussy rumbled and throbbed underneath the dick, the orgasmic vibrations coming up through it all the way to the tip, giving it life. The feel of it shaking in my mouth was unbelievable.

I let go of it and lay back on the bed. Consuela leaned over and kissed me. "Good girls get presents," she said, licking my earlobe. "Turn over, baby."

I rolled over and got up on my knees, lifting my ass in the air, expecting Consuela to fuck my pussy from behind like usual. She stood up, and I watched her juice up the dildo, then put on a glove and squirt another helping of lube into her hand. She came back to the bed and started rubbing my asshole with her gloved fingers, until one, then two, then three were inside it, loosening it. When they were moving in and out easily she removed them and put the tip of her cock there, moving slow, little by little, easing it inside.

I was a virgin that way, trembling and scared like a little girl. It felt so good and so scary I started crying. My asshole relaxed completely, letting Consuela's dick slide in and out, exploring the incredible tightness and sensitivity. "Is it good, baby?" Consuela asked.

"Yes," I sputtered, sobbing with joy. "Yes."

It was our new thing now, sucking and ass fucking.

It definitely tipped the scale back in Consuela's favor.

⊹

Sex was getting almost boring with Consuela and Leif together. Consuela was totally different in that setting. She seemed almost insecure, and I didn't like seeing that side of her. The way she had to control everything got to be a real turn-off. Still, there were amazing moments, like when me and Consuela were 69ing, and Leif came up behind one then the other of us, fucking us in turn.

The cuddling was the best, going to the movies and snuggling up together, taking turns being in the middle; our dinners out, laughing and talking about our jobs, our plans, our ideas. We got to be best friends over that summer, and I loved both of them dearly, but with the sex, I was in way over my head.

"Do you ever feel bad?" I asked Leif one night in his bed, curled across his chest, playing with his nipples.

"No," he answered without hesitation.

"But we're lying."

"She has no right to deny us. Besides, it would just hurt her."

"But doesn't lying hurt her worse?"

"Not if she doesn't find out."

"What if she does?"

"She won't."

But she did.

⧫

Consuela was supposed to be two hours away, visiting her sick mother. Her sister had called the night before, saying it was an emergency, and to come home right away. Leif gave her the keys to his Saab, kissed her, wished her a safe trip, then called me.

I got there at seven, right after work. It was Friday. Consuela would be gone for at least the weekend, he said. Just you and me, here, all weekend. We'll never leave the bed, he said, and we didn't, until Saturday night when Consuela walked in on us.

It was way after dinner, but we had just gotten around to ordering some food. We were naked, had been since the night before, nothing but sex, sleep, more sex, more sleep. The delivery man brought the Chinese we had called in.

I opened the noodles, brown and juicy and lukewarm. I was hungry, but not just for food. Leif was sitting on the edge of the bed. I knelt down, facing him, the noodles wide open like a mouth. Leif was soft, so I took him in my hand and licked him until he got hard and solid. Then I gently turned his dick downward and plunged it into the noodles, stirring them with it.

"Mmmm," he whispered. "Those are delicious." I put the container down and started licking the sauce off his cock, salty and sweet mixed together. I was sucking hard, pumping with my hand, Leif's ass tensing and lifting as I went. I was vaguely aware of Leif trying to pull away at one point, but I was so involved, so hungry, that I held on, then something was grabbing me by the hair, pulling me off, hurting me.

Consuela was screaming in my face, slapping me hard over and over again. I fell back and she climbed on top of me, yelling, bitch, fucking asshole, hate, kill, lying, cheating whore. I put my face over my hands, to protect it, but also not to look at her.

Fortunately, Leif was stronger than she was, and he got her off me and wrapped his arms around her, holding her tight, like a parent restraining a child in the middle of a tantrum.

She went limp in his embrace, and while she sobbed in his arms, I got dressed and let myself out.

⊹

Consuela never spoke to me again, though I had dinner with Leif one more time.

He called me at work, asked me to meet him at the Italian restaurant where we'd all gone the first time.

"Why?" I asked. "Why'd you call?"

"I wanted to explain," he said.

"OK," I said. I'd tried to call Consuela several times, but she wouldn't speak with me or call me back. I was too scared to show my face at her door. I hadn't tried to contact Leif.

"She's complicated," he said.

"No kidding," I said. I saw Leif blush for the first time. He looked down into his plate and ran his fork through the strands of pasta there. "Is she going to be okay?"

"Yes," he said.

"Is she going to forgive me?"

"No," he said.

I wanted to hit him, punch him, push him out of the way so I could have Consuela back. "Why?" I asked. "Why you and not me?"

He shook his head. "She needs me."

"What does that make me?" I was crying, in public, I didn't care.

Leif gave no answer, just held my hand, kindly, tenderly. He brought it to his lips and kissed it. "Call me if you need anything," he said.

"I can't fuck you anymore, Leif."

"That's not what I meant," he said.

I stopped crying and looked around the restaurant, filled with people eating, laughing, socializing, working, living. "Okay," I said, but I knew I wouldn't.

We hugged for a long time on the sidewalk.

Then I walked into the night, breathing the lethargic, steamy air of late summer, the edge of autumn in its heaviness.

Beached

I hate the beach. Sand sliding between toes feels creepy to me. I step lightly, because you never know when you're going to hit a jagged shell or a hard rock. The water is always freezing, and the waves touch your bare skin before it's ready. Even if you go in little by little, you can't avoid the shock. As for the salt water, I never let my mouth get close enough to taste it. Most of all, the ocean scares me, with its tides that come and go, the eternities of mysterious creatures teeming inside it, and its silent, powerful relationship with the moon.

The beach is the last place I expected to meet you. Do you want to know what I was doing the hour before we found each other outside of Susan's little house, that everyone said would erode into the ocean before long? I was locked in one of the three bedrooms there, squeezing the striped Peruvian bedspread in my fists like it was one of those stress balls, sweating hard, right through my white tank top and the wraparound skirt that Susan bought me on one of her business trips to the far East. Behind the door, I listened to the Rolling Stones and the sounds of drunk people laughing. Through the window,

I watched the moonlight and the tall pines that hugged the house, their branches wavering, the motion shy yet loaded, nearly imperceptible, like my lips just before you kissed me.

I hate parties, too, and had tried to convince Susan not to have one. It was James who broke my reverie, cranking the doorknob in vain, then banging his fist on the aging wood. "Hey," he called, sounding like the lush he is. "Who's in there?" I let go of the bedspread, glancing at the two bunched-up lumps of fabric created by my squeezing hands. They looked obscene, maybe because of what I knew was about to happen in there. I walked to the doorway and opened it. James was with a woman I didn't know, most likely one of the tourists Susan was always chatting up on the strip and inviting over for wildness and adventure. It was another thing she did that I hated, but how can I blame her now?

James lunged into the room, dragging the giggling woman by her wrist. I was barely gone before he dove his face into her breasts. I didn't bother closing the door behind me. Someone, maybe Susan, would be joining them.

The living room was like a beehive, swarming and dark and dripping with sweet, ripe smells. Susan, the queen, was sitting on the tattered couch, hiking up her dress and opening her legs for a man I didn't know. As he lowered his face onto her crotch the tip of his tongue wagged eagerly, anticipating her wet clit. I felt the flash of jealousy I always felt when Susan made it with someone else. No matter how I tried, I just couldn't rise above it.

Lila sat on the couch next to Susan, pinching her nipples, stroking the man's head while he drank from Susan's pussy. The party was moving into orgy stage, always my cue to leave, even though it meant walking the beach. But how can I complain?

I walked down the private stretch of beach, away from any lights and commotion, the night sky over it deep black. You were lying on the sand, staring into the sky's dark glory which, unlike the beach, I have always loved. I didn't know what you were looking at, only that you were concentrating hard, because you didn't hear me approaching. I stopped and turned my eyes in the direction yours were looking, at the white stars, the pearly moon. My anxious heart settled a bit.

You startled me with your hands wrapping around my waist from behind. I didn't even hear you rise up from your bed of coarse, damp sand. You must have floated, like an angel, or a ghost. But you were real, your hands big and warm on my body.

I should have yelled, but I couldn't, or just plain didn't. Instead I looked at your white hands cupped at my navel, kneading the bow that help my skirt together. I had tied it loosely, just hours before. I hadn't put anything on underneath it. Your fingers played with the bow tenderly. Your fingers played with it tenderly. I watched them, slipping into and out of the two uneven loops, stroking the tails, pulling them gently until they released. The skirt fell soundlessly onto the matted sand. I peered down, transfixed by the sight of your fingertips brushing my bare belly, almost tickling me, teasing my wiry, black pubic hair. I moved my feet apart, just enough for my legs to be open, enough to separate the lips of my pussy, enough to feel the air brush me there.

It was exquisite, but nothing compared to your hand, sliding full palm down my skin, curving to follow the path to my cunt, covering it with sweaty heat. You pressed there, pulling me back toward your body, which was big and muscular and tall. My frizzy hair brushed your neck as your fingers danced carefully between my legs. I pushed back to feel your cock press into my cheeks. Your shorts were between your skin and mine. I didn't want it that way, I wanted your cock pressed into my crack while your fingers slid in and out of my pussy.

I reached behind and pulled. The shorts slipped down easily, far enough, anyway, to let me feel you, your wrinkly, slippery foreskin sliding as you began to move your hips, swaying with me to the rhythm of your finger fucking. You placed your thumb on my clit, sliding the hood loose, building a wave inside me. I stared into the ocean, watching those waves roll toward me, pushing with a completely reliable, unstoppable rhythm until each one expired on the shore. Your fingers fucked me harder, and I came, and felt you come, too, warm liquid like manna on my butt cheeks. I relaxed, breathed, moved my hips to spread your come on my skin.

Then we both stood still, holding each other, my arms awkwardly trying to reach backwards to wrap around you, your thick waist, your firm stomach. You felt delicious. I knew I should turn to look at you, but I was afraid to lose the knowledge of your body, the primitive, wordless, pure fucking. I began to think this is what Susan wants, with all her fucking and orgies, something perfect and ancient and frightening, like the waves, the ocean—like the moon.

I looked up into it, its glimmering roundness ruthless and beautiful. You stepped back and slowly turned me around, your hands guiding my waist until we faced each other. You were smiling at me like you knew me, and you leaned into my face and kissed my full lips with your thin ones. When you breathed hard into my ear I could feel your mouth curved into a smile.

The night was young. We spent it together on the beach. You even got me in the water, then licked the ocean off my breasts, my belly, my legs and feet, sucked it from my pussy until I came in your mouth time after time. I took it from you, too, salt and sweetness from your cock exploding in my throat. Do you know how much I loved it?

When we got home just before the sun rose, Susan was sleeping, naked in our bed with the strange woman and James. You stepped in quietly behind me, and we were standing there, in a staggered vertical row, as Susan's groggy eyes opened and looked at us. She saw me first, and smiled. I felt my love for her swell. She beckoned with her head, and I dropped my shirt and skirt on the floor and climbed into bed, pushing James and the woman out of the way so I could hold Susan. She kissed me, then whispered to you to come in, too. You sat on the edge of the bed with your clothes on, stroking the hair of the other woman until she opened her eyes. "Hi," you said, and she tried to smile at you but she couldn't, then she jumped up and we heard her retching in the bathroom.

Susan played with my breasts, twisting and sucking the nipples, while you watched. She tried to pull you in, but you said no, and held her head while she sucked me. I looked at you while she did me. I watched you watch me come, your hand holding Susan's head the whole time she worked me with her mouth. Nothing ever looked as lovely as you did, watching me orgasm in the first morning light.

After, Susan rolled off and lit a cigarette. She looked bored and tired, picking my pubic hairs from her teeth. James snored and fell off the bed. Your girlfriend stumbled out of the bathroom, dressed and ready to go. You nestled a piece of paper in my hand as you left.

I pushed Susan away and went into the kitchen to make coffee.

Mrs. M.:
A Case of Female Hysteria

D r. Fleisher treated many patients suffering from female hysteria. It was his specialty. Women came from miles away for the unique relief offered by his expert, practiced massage therapies. Besides being a successful physician, he was a happily married man, his wife dutifully opening her legs on a regular, weekly basis. It was enough for him, and for her, too, at least since he agreed to perform pelvic massage on her after the act, and especially since he'd secured for her one of the special, state-of-the-art instruments which had recently made his job so much easier.

Because of all this, Mrs. Manning came as a complete surprise. He first laid eyes on her in the waiting room, white gloved hands clutching her bag, dabbing at her forehead with an embroidered handkerchief. Her hat—a hideous, ornate combination of straw, ruffles, flowers, and red feathers—rested on the chair beside her. In the midst of the cacophonous ornamentation, a stuffed bluebird perched, mouth slightly open. Dr. Fleisher cringed. He despised the new hat fashions, in particular those with birds. There was something terrible about such beautiful, free creatures being placed atop women's heads.

Although he was a general practitioner and saw all sorts of maladies, he could identify female hysteria on sight. Mrs. Manning's perfectly configured hair twist, her impeccably powdered face, the way she pulled at the standing collar of her long dress—all that coupled with nervous fiddling with her hair and wiping of her brow told him immediately that this was female hysteria in the extreme.

He sighed as he let the patient before her out. He really did feel for these women, and derived satisfaction from his ability to help them, but something always troubled him about it. After the paroxysm which indicated the treatment had been successful, the woman was always relaxed, smiling, and grateful, while he felt a strange depression, even mild embarrassment. He never understood why, and didn't dwell on it. It was his job to help and heal. Focusing on unusual feelings which inevitably passed would only lead to the kind of hysteria from which his patients suffered.

He greeted Mrs. Manning, offering a handshake. "Hello, doctor," she said, her hand twitching slightly, hesitating, then jerking out as though in spasm. It crashed into his palm, passing it roughly and landing on his forearm. "I'm so sorry," she stammered, reaching back to properly shake his hand.

Her grip was unexpectedly firm, and it made Dr. Fleisher pause. He had always been a man who put stock in handshakes and the determination of character and personality they offered. Mrs. Manning's was not the handshake of a hysterical woman, or a weak one. He put that aside, in order not to confuse his initial impression, which based on every other clue, was stunningly accurate. "Come in, Mrs. Manning," he said.

As he slipped behind his dark, imposing desk, Mrs. Manning seated herself in the maroon leather chair on its other side, falling into the same proper, controlled position she'd assumed in the waiting area. Dr. Fleisher began the interview, and quickly verified that he'd been right. He listed headaches, sleeplessness, irritability, and wandering thoughts as symptoms. "What sorts of thoughts?" he asked, running his hand over his nearly bald head. It was late in the day, he was tired, it was sweating.

Mrs. Manning's face flushed pink. She cast her gaze downward and wrung the embroidered handkerchief as though she could squeeze something out of it. She whispered. "They creep into my mind at the most terrible times. When I'm sewing, or serving tea. Sometimes when I'm looking at my child." This last one seemed to particularly disturb her. She choked back a sob and looked up, her face desperate, her black eyes shining like hot coals against her white skin, pale and radiant as moonlight.

A hollow feeling twanged inside him, like the deep, doleful plucking of a cello. He was taken aback, and moved. "Mrs. Manning." He spoke her name softly. "Perhaps you need a different sort of doctor."

She lifted one hand in the air, fingers waving like the wings of a canary. "No," she cried, then settled herself. "Mrs. Peony recommended you so highly."

Her voice trailed off and she dropped her head again. "Very well," said Dr. Fleisher. The pang of longing he felt was evolving, collecting layers of other feelings. He had no choice but to ignore them.

He stood up and opened the door to the examining room. "Step in here," he said. "And undress from the waist down. There's a blanket on the examining table."

"That's all?" she asked, and paused.

He looked at her linen dress, dusky rose, wrapped tight around her cinched waist, falling in pleats and layers around her lower body, hiding its natural shape. His wife complained bitterly of the discomfort caused by the layers of garments she had to wear. She especially hated the corset, which strangled her breasts and chest. But there was no need for Mrs. Manning to take it off. Dr. Fleisher felt himself redden and begin to sputter. "Yes," he forced himself to say, evenly and easily. "Yes."

⊹

In a few minutes, Dr. Fleisher knocked on the door of the examining room. "Come in," Mrs. Manning called.

He found her sitting on the edge of the table. She had taken off the long skirt of her dress, but left the bodice with the high, lacy collar. Her graceful, curved arms rested at each side of her like wings. Her bare hands sat unmoving in her lap. They looked soft and comfortable, the nails trimmed and neat.

She had neglected to unfold the blanket. The square it made barely covered her ample hips, and ended mid-thigh, so he could see her legs dangling lazily, and her pampered looking feet. Before he could stop the thought, he found himself thinking that she looked lovely. It horrified him. He had certainly found other hysterics attractive, but it was always an objective observation. "Mrs. Manning," he whispered hoarsely, "Unfold the blanket and lie down." He turned his head, listening to the sounds of Mrs. Manning shifting her body and the blanket into place. When silence fell, he said, "Ready?"

"Yes," she answered.

Her eyes were closed as if in rapture, the lids fluttering almost imperceptibly, her lips parted, pink and moist. Dr. Fleisher walked to the foot of the table and seated himself, then unfolded the stirrups so they jutted out of each corner of the table like arms. "Move down," he said. Mrs. Manning scooted her body closer, opening her eyes so she could see. "Put your feet here," said Dr. Fleisher, pointing to the stirrups.

One foot, then the other peeked out from the edge of the blanket, landing perfectly in the wooden containers. Dr. Fleisher's head was right between them, and up close, he saw that they were the smoothest, most perfect feet he had ever laid eyes on.

He pushed the blanket backwards, so that it draped over Mrs. Manning's knees, between her legs, shrouding every part of her but those pretty feet. Even though technological improvements had enhanced pelvic massage treatments considerably, shortening their duration and providing greater relief for the patient, Dr. Fleisher found himself reaching for a jar. Mrs. Manning's legs twitched erratically as he dipped his fingers into the warm, slick, scented oil. He put his other hand on the blanket, finding her knee and squeezing it. "Relax, now, Mrs. Manning." He reached into the darkness under the blanket, searching until he found the place between Mrs. Manning's legs.

When he began to touch her, she stopped twitching. Dr. Fleisher felt her body sink into the table, her deep sighs urging his fingers to continue, keep rubbing the flesh around her vaginal lips, then the lips themselves, covering the whole area with lubrication, making pressing, circular, tapping motions.

Dr. Fleisher had been trained, of course, but he found that over the years it was important to expand his techniques, and so he experimented freely, with great results. It was meditative for him, in a way, closing his eyes as he worked, feeling the response of the woman, allowing it to guide his hands and fingers. Mrs. Manning's sighs grew deeper, she began moaning, moving her lower body in the primal, rhythmic way that indicated paroxysm would soon occur.

It didn't, however. Despite that, she was clearly achieving deep relaxation, so Dr. Fleisher continued the massage with his fingers rather than reaching for an instrument. He determined that her hysteria was so severe that the extended treatment was called for.

He pulled away each time Mrs. Manning neared paroxysm, seeking to lengthen the treatment, falling into reverie with her, his hand and her hips in perfect rhythm. Suddenly her hand was on his, pushing it lower. She was whispering something. Dr. Fleisher felt so feverish he could hardly understand her, then the words "Put it inside," came to him, as if on the air, floating in the room, not connected to either one of them, and his finger slipped into the wet opening of her vagina and began moving in and out with the rhythm of her hips, one finger, then another, then one more, feeling the dark, mysterious cavern. Somehow Dr. Fleisher knew she was touching herself but it was a fact that was detached from him, like the words "Put it inside" that floated in the room separate from Mrs. Manning or himself, then Mrs. Manning's body began to shake and tremble and writhe in the biggest paroxysm Dr. Fleisher had ever witnessed. He felt the rumbling and throbbing with his hands. He knew the paroxysm occurred inside the vagina, but he had never actually felt the juices flush downward. It fascinated and excited him, from a medical point of view. He stood up, wiped his hand on a cotton cloth, and told Mrs. Manning to get dressed, showing himself out without looking at her.

⦀

The next time Mrs. Manning came in, Dr. Fleisher determined that weekly treatments were in order. For a month, he continued massage therapy, with his hands and with the vibrating instruments, aided by Mrs. Manning herself. Masturbation proved how depraved Mrs. Manning's hysteria had rendered her. Yet Dr. Fleisher couldn't help but take advantage of the opportunity it offered to glean new information and learn new techniques. He had never had such a receptive patient, and he didn't waste the opportunity for research. With his hand exploring her inner and outer vagina, he made note of the physiological changes that occurred during paroxysms, and marveled at how intense and full body they could be. In the interests of medicine, he deemed visuals necessary, and he began to watch Mrs. Manning during the treatments, noting the way the vaginal lips grew larger with stimulation, how pink and swollen she became, how the opening bloomed like a flower, inviting his fingers or the instrument to enter.

He even discovered that Mrs. Manning could achieve paroxysm more than once. Many times, in fact. She would lie on the table, her feet tensing in the stirrups, toes squeezing them hard and fast, writhing and lifting her hips up and down, her body shaking until she fell into the most extreme state of relaxation he had ever seen.

The ramifications for treating female hysteria were astounding. He saw an important, well-received paper coming out of this.

One aspect of the treatments shamed him, but he put it aside for the greater good. It was true that he had to relieve himself in the bathroom after she left, rubbing his penis back and forth until white liquid spurted into the toilet bowl. It was an inevitable if unfortunate result of the research he was conducting. Despite the shame, he hadn't been so excited or interested in anything since medical school.

One week, after her third paroxysm, Mrs. Manning tossed the blanket aside so Dr. Fleisher could see the entire bottom half of her body, the lush buttocks lifting and lowering, the hips undulating as if swimming through warm, soothing water. She was treating herself with one of Dr. Fleisher's instruments. He stood beside the table, taking notes, watching her uninhibitedly rub the buzzing instrument all over her vagina, the thick cord streaming from its end like a long, obscene tail.

She looked enraptured, her head tipped back, revealing her long swan-like neck, mouth open, emitting sounds that came from deep inside her being. Dr. Fleisher wondered, for a moment, whether his wife found this pleasure with the instrument he had given her, whether she would allow him to take her this far. Mrs. Manning's paroxysms wrenched at her very soul, releasing its tension and darkness in powerful waves. Dr. Fleisher was convinced the cure for female hysteria could be absolute with treatments like this. Mrs. Manning herself, one of the most extreme cases he had ever seen, was already showing consistent progress.

Another paroxysm, and Mrs. Manning turned her head to the side, panting, looking at him. "Dr. Fleisher," she said. "It's not enough."

"All right," he said, putting down his papers and reaching for the instrument.

"No," she said. "I need more. If you want to cure me, there has to be more."

"Twice a week?" he asked, unnerved by the sight of her half naked body, her legs flopped open without reservation, displaying her wet, throbbing vagina.

She shook her head. "I have to bare everything," She wrapped her arms around her chest, closing her eyes. "I'll never get better holding it in."

Something stirred in Dr. Fleisher, a small, quick flutter that immediately choked itself. He felt the bulge in his pants grow. "All right," he said in his most clinical voice.

Mrs. Manning sat up and reached behind her to unbutton the bodice of her deep blue dress. Dr. Fleisher watched as she pulled it off, then undid the suffocating corset, releasing the round voluptuousness of her breasts. The sight of the erect nipples made Dr. Fleisher's breath catch in his throat. He never saw his wife's breasts. He barely saw her body. The feelings of longing he experienced the first day he met Mrs. Manning returned, washing over him, making him breathe hard and fast.

Dr. Fleisher reached for Mrs. Manning's nipples, trembling and touching, his palms folding around the whole of Mrs. Manning's breasts, cushiony but firm, like an expensive pillow, and before he knew it his mouth was on them and he was licking and sucking, weeping like a baby, and somewhere in the background he heard the buzzing sound of the vibrating instrument, and when Mrs. Manning experienced yet another paroxysm, one that made her scream and cry out like a wolf during a full moon, Dr. Fleisher felt his own penis erupt, spilling hot, creamy liquid inside his pants.

⊹

Mrs. Manning shook his hand vigorously when she left, thanking him profusely for his dedication to his profession, expressing profound gratitude for the vast improvement in her condition. He watched her turn away from him, the horrible dead bluebird on her head going with her, her long woolen cape swinging around her as she walked.

◈

The treatments increased to twice a week. Because of the absolute necessity of conducting them without limitation on sound or anything else, Dr. Fleisher moved them to a hotel. He found that Mrs. Manning was even more relaxed in that setting, and that the treatments achieved even greater results, which led him to theorize that female hysteria should perhaps be treated in a more homelike environment than a doctor's office.

Mrs. Manning continued to prefer full body nakedness, and without the table and stirrups, felt free to assume a variety of positions. Her favorite, and the most effective, found her on hands and knees, buttocks jutting into the air like satin-covered hills. In this position, the combination of fingers moving in and out of the inner vagina while the vibrating instrument massaged the outer vagina achieved the most profound paroxysms.

Mrs. Manning would leave the treatments in a heightened state of relaxation and happiness. Dr. Fleisher remained behind to clean up. He had learned to bring an extra pair of trousers to replace the soiled ones.

Things were going well, beyond his wildest imaginings. He had prepared several pages and was putting a stunning paper together. Although Mrs. Manning had improved to almost normalcy, Dr. Fleisher hesitated to end treatments. He had already found the cure for female hysteria, but with Mrs. Manning, nuances and details were turning up all the time. Certainly continued treatment would result in no harm.

One week, she arrived at the hotel in a highly agitated state. It was a snowy night, and white, wet flakes covered her brown hair and the brown fur of her cape's collar as she entered and sank into the leather chair in the corner, her face buried in her hands.

"What is it?" asked Dr. Fleisher, his heart pounding.

She looked at him plaintively, a tear falling from her dark eye. "Will you hold me?"

Dr. Fleisher felt uncomfortable. This was not his role, yet Mrs. Manning's sadness touched him. She removed her cape and gloves, tossed them wearily aside, and reached out for him like a hurt child. He went to her, falling to his knees and taking her in his arms.

She wept there, her salty tears wetting the side of his head, her hot breath falling in gasps into his ear. She began to kiss him, his earlobe, his cheek, his forehead, eyes, and chin, then took his face in her hands and began kissing him on the mouth, opening it wide, her tongue finding his tongue, moving against it, asking for return.

Dr. Fleisher had never been kissed this way, except for once when his colleagues at medical school bought him a prostitute for his birthday. It had released an ache in him he didn't know existed, and he had cried like a baby as the prostitute kissed him deeply, and did other things to him that no one had done before or since.

Now, he found himself back there, remembering how it felt to be young and afraid, realizing the feeling had never gone away, only become balanced by other things, his authority, his knowledge, his confidence in his work. Finding himself thus vulnerable, he let professionalism fall away, welcoming Mrs. Manning's tongue in his mouth.

"Come," she whispered in his ear, standing up, pulling off dress, corset, undergarments, landing naked on the bed.

He undressed, folding his woolen suit and placing it neatly on the chair, and joined her. He looked quite different than he did on that night years ago, also in a hotel, when he was young, thick blonde hair falling in waves around his head, broad shoulders, flat, strong belly and firm buttocks and thighs. He had been told he was handsome, and when he proposed to his wife she giggled nervously, and ran to tell her friends before even giving him her answer. That came after the prostitute. He had hoped lovemaking with his wife would be something like that, but it never was, and he understood that he had been naïve and foolish to expect a woman of decency to behave that way.

Yet he did not find Mrs. Manning indecent. In fact, he found her searching eyes, the complexity of her emotions, and the freedom of her physicality to be profoundly courageous. This courage, he concluded, was the key to cure, and in that moment, he understood that he, too, had manifested the condition underlying the veneer of female hysteria—loneliness, and the desire to be seen openly by another human being.

Mrs. Manning touched him, running her hands along his slumped, tired shoulders, over the graying hair on his chest, the flab of his paunch. He closed his eyes, submitting.

His penis stood hard and erect. Silently, he prayed that she would do what he could not ask her to do, and she did, she bent low and took him in her mouth, sucked him vigorously until he burst, then knelt over him so her sex was in his mouth, and he tasted its sweet, musky flavor, so like the earth, and his mind began to show him visions of his boyhood, playing in mud, hands and arms slathered with wet goo, lying in the sun in a field, bringing red, fragrant flowers to his nose, crushing their delicate petals to his face.

When Mrs. Manning finally climbed off and lay beside him, he was hard again, and she got on top of him, slipping him inside her, riding him like a horse, images of merry go rounds in his head, fanciful, joyous ponies flying through the air.

He came.

Mrs. Manning dismounted and dressed, crying quietly. She approached Dr. Fleisher, lying in stillness and awe, kissed him gently on the lips, and showed herself out.

⊹

That was the last appointment Dr. Fleisher had with Mrs. Manning. She did not show up for treatment the next week, or the next, or the next.

When he called, he found her telephone was disconnected. Further inquiries revealed that she had moved to another state with her husband and family. Dr. Fleisher walked around in a trance, never touching his wife, who never asked what was wrong.

After a month, he took his fifty-one pages and burned them one by one, watching them curl into black ash in the fireplace, smoke rushing up the chimney, whispering cruel things in his ear as it went.

He continued to treat female hysteria in his office with the requisite instruments, and eventually he and his wife returned to their weekly lovemaking, and normalcy.

Occasionally, when his colleagues talked about hysteria and made jokes about his success in treating it, he would remember Mrs. Manning and the burned pages. Sometimes, when he watched his wife as he massaged her with the newest vibrating instrument, he would see glimpses of Mrs. Manning's passion, but they were fleeting.

Now and then, after a dream of Mrs. Manning's mouth loving him, he would wake breathless and sweating, his penis painful and hard, and he would clamp down on it with his hand until the ache passed.